Booklist (January 1, 2010 (Vol. 106, No. 9))

Grades 8–11. The first half of this tense and compelling novel treads familiar ground: the catch-22 of bullying. Fifteen-year-old Sami, whose father was born in Iran, is regularly harassed by a group of guys who call him a sand monkey. But if he turns them in not only will the beatings worsen but there could be fallout for his family, too—his strict father has worked so hard to become a respected part of the community. The escalating violence at school increases the stress at home; his father now ignores Sami even when they pray together. Stratton's grasp of daily Muslim life brings freshness to this story line before unleashing a whole new hell: a late-night FBI raid that implicates Sami's father in an international terror ring known as the Brotherhood of Martyrs. Stratton's ever-readable prose is peppered with Sami's believable inner dialogue, and the social fallout, plot twists, and even Sami's renewed interest in his religion all feel authentic. A fast, exciting read with weighty underpinnings.

Borderline

ALLAN STRATTON

An Imprint of HarperCollins*Publishers*

HarperTeen is an imprint of HarperCollins Publishers.

Borderline
www.harperteen.com

Library of Congress Cataloging-in-Publication Data
Stratton, Allan.
Borderline / Allan Stratton. — 1st ed.
p. cm.
Summary: Despite the strained relationship between them,
teenaged Sami Sabiri risks his life to uncover the truth when his
father is implicated in a terrorist plot.
ISBN 978-0-06-145111-9 (trade bdg.)
ISBN 978-0-06-145112-6 (lib. bdg.)
[1. Fathers and sons—Fiction. 2. Identity—Fiction.
3. Prejudices—Fiction. 4. Friendship—Fiction. 5. Muslims—
Fiction. 6. Terrorism—Fiction. 7. Iranian Americans—Fiction.]
I. Title.
PZ7.S9109Bor 2010   2009005241
[Fic]—dc22   CIP
                                              AC

Typography by Alison Klapthor

11 12 13 14   LP/RRDB   10 9 8 7 6 5

First Edition

For Faizal, Laila, and Azeem

PART ONE

PART ONE

One

I'm next door in Andy's driveway, shooting hoops with him and Marty. The holidays are over next week, and we've hardly been together at all. Andy was in summer school for Math all July. After that, he and his family took Marty to their cottage on the Canadian side of the Thousand Islands. They just got back yesterday.

I could have gone too, except for Dad. Other times he's let me, but when he heard that Mr. and Mrs. J wouldn't be there 24/7, he pulled the plug. "You're too young to handle the responsibility," he said.

"What responsibility?" I demanded. "We'll be swimming. Fishing. Dad, please. I'm almost sixteen."

"I've said what I've said."

Yeah, and it's totally not fair. I don't do drugs. I hate booze. And that stuff with Mary Louise Prescott happened over a year ago.

The worst was watching the videos Andy and Marty e-mailed of them hiking, swimming, and cannonballing off the Johnsons' dock. They even got to take the boat out on their own. "So, Sammy, what are *you* doing?" They laughed as they hot-dogged through the islands.

But now they're back and everything's fantastic.

At least it *was*. Dad's stepped onto our verandah. The day's been a scorcher, but it seems nobody's told him. Even home, after dinner, it's like he's still at work, supervising the microbe researchers at the lab. His jacket's off, but he's wearing everything else: silk tie, dress shirt, pearl cuff links, and flannels.

I tense as he stands by the railing, watching us play. I was doing great. Now I suck.

"Close, very close," Dad says, as my third shot in a row rockets off the backboard.

I get the basketball before it bounces into the street, pass to Andy, and fix Dad with a stare. "You want something?"

"Can your mother and I borrow you for a while?" Translation: It's time for prayers. Years ago, Mom convinced Dad to give me prayer calls in code, so I wouldn't be embarrassed in front of my friends. But Andy and Marty know the drill.

"You need me this second?"

"Not right away. But, say, in five minutes?" Dad flashes his fake smile, the one where his lips go stiff. "Sorry to interrupt your game."

Go, Dad. Just Go. I shoot out imaginary force fields, picture him flying through the air into tomorrow, but he hangs around like a bad fart.

"You boys have grown this summer!" he says out of nowhere. Dad makes stupid announcements like this almost every time he sees us. It's his idea of Taking An Interest. Well, if he really took an interest, he'd know Andy's been six feet tall since ninth grade; the guys call him Stiltz. And Marty doesn't grow up, just out. Fries, Cokes, chips. If he keeps at it, he'll turn into his parents.

Dad waits for one of us to break the silence. We don't. He bobbles his head like a dashboard ornament, gives us a tight little wave, and finally—*finally*—goes back inside.

We play a bit more, but it's not the same.

Dad taps on the living room window. When he was a kid, he fled Iran because of the secret police. So what did he learn about freedom? Not much, apparently. I can't even shoot a private game of hoops with my friends.

"Catch you later," I say.

I take off my shoes and socks inside the front door, wash my hands, face, and feet in the hall bathroom, and head to the family room. I'm expecting Mom and Dad to be standing by the prayer rugs, waiting. Instead they're sitting on the leather sectional, eating grapes, and the rugs are rolled up on their shelves under the flat-screen TV. Mom's green silk hijab is folded loosely on top; she only wears it at mosque and prayers—a big relief, as far as I'm concerned.

"What's up?"

Mom's eyes dance to the ceiling the way they do when there's exciting news. Dad pats the cushion next to him. "I don't only call you in for prayers," he says. I hate how he reads my mind. Does he know what I say to Andy and Marty?

I sit on the edge of the seat, take a paper napkin from beside the fruit bowl, and twist it gently in my fingers.

"You want to tell him?" Dad asks Mom.

"No, no, it was your idea." Mom always likes to make Dad look good.

He rubs his thumb against his ring. "End of September, I'm off to a four-day security conference in Toronto.

I'll be leading a seminar Friday afternoon, and touring their new category-four lab Monday morning. But I can skip the weekend workshops." He looks at Mom as if he's not sure what he's supposed to say next.

"Your Dad noticed the Toronto hockey team . . . ," Mom prompts.

"Yes, the Leafs," he says. "They've got a preview with the New York Islanders, Friday night. Baseball's in town too: The Jays have a doubleheader Saturday with Boston." He takes a deep breath. "I can get us tickets through the conference organizers."

I lean forward, the napkin tight between my hands. "*Us*? You can get *us* tickets?"

"Not *us*," Mom bats the air with her hand. "Just you and your Dad. I couldn't be dragged kicking and screaming."

I smile. Whenever there's sports on TV, even playoffs, Mom leaves Dad and me for a bubble bath or to squirrel away with a book. The exception is golf. She'll watch that crap for hours. Go figure.

"We'd be flying out of Rochester early Friday morning, coming back late afternoon Monday, Inshallah," Dad says. "You'll be missing two days of school, but I'm sure I can make arrangements with the Academy."

Two days off school? Has Dad had a brain transplant?

"We haven't done anything special for quite a while," he continues. "I was thinking a father–son weekend would be nice. That is, if you're interested."

I'm interested, sure—in having two days off school to see baseball and hockey. But the father–son part, that's scary. It's bad enough when Dad and I are alone watching TV. We sit on opposite ends of the sectional, like there's this invisible border between our cushions and we're in totally different countries that don't talk to each other, or even speak the same language. When there's a commercial and somebody should say something, one of us leaves for a snack or a pee. So to go all Friday through Monday, with just the two of us . . .

Dad sees me hesitate. "Of course, you and your friends . . . You may have plans."

"Maybe. I don't know. They just got back."

He takes a deep breath. "I understand."

Mom shoots me a look: *Your father's trying.*

I know and I'm being a shit and I hate myself. But I can't help it. Before Mary Louise Prescott, things were normal. Dad could be fun. He'd tease me, and I'd laugh. Even when I messed up, we could talk. I wasn't just a disappointment.

Dad stares awkwardly at the sliding patio doors. Our backyard faces the Meadowvale Country Club. Through the glass, I can see the sun touching the row of maples that line the fourteenth fairway. "Time for prayers," he says quietly. His shoulders wilt.

I can't stand it. "Dad," I hear myself say. "About the weekend. Why don't I just say yes?"

He looks at me like he's not sure he heard right. "You want to come?"

I nod. "Sure, I guess. Yeah. I can do stuff with Andy and Marty anytime."

A smile rolls over his face. His chest swells. His fingers stretch.

Oh my god, is he gonna hug me? Am I supposed to hug *him*?

From the look on Dad's face, he doesn't know what to do either. He clears his throat, claps his hands, and goes to the prayer rugs.

Whew, that was close!

Two

After prayers, Andy drives us to Mr. Softy's in the Deathmobile, aka his Mom's old Camry. We call it the Deathmobile because of all the scrapes it's been in. Mrs. J thinks parking lots are expressways, and she's not so great on curbs. Andy inherited it last fall when he got his permit. Since he turned seventeen, top of the summer, he's had his full license. Now he's free as a bird, meaning we are too.

We eat our cones, propped against the hood. I brag about my trip with Dad. The guys are jealous about the tickets, but they don't let me off easy.

"Your dad was gonna hug you?" Andy gasps. "What, and get his shirt dirty?"

"I knew I shouldn't have told you."

Marty laughs. "You could've picked up spores from his lab. Started glowing in the dark."

"Funny, Marty. Original too."

We toss our cone wrappings in the garbage bin and head to the small neighborhood park across the street, where we sit on the ledge of the fountain, dangle our feet in the water, and chill.

Andy and Marty have been my best friends since fourth grade. Before them, I didn't have any friends, period. Our mosque is a half-hour drive away in Rochester, so I never got to hang out with the kids from my Saturday morning madrassa. And at public school, I never fit in. There was this little clique that used to point at me and make bomb sounds. At recess, I'd stay inside and pretend to nap. The teachers didn't say anything.

Things changed when Andy arrived. It was a Saturday. I was nine, lying on my belly, staring at this anthill by our curb, when a moving van pulled in next door. Men hauled boxes and furniture, and a woman yelled, "Fine, just don't go far," at this skinny kid in a Bart Simpson T-shirt who was running around the yard like his pants were on fire.

In a flash, Skinny disappeared. I figured he'd blasted

off to Mars or something, and went back to watching the ants drag a grasshopper head into their colony. Next thing I knew, there was a pair of sneakers in front of my face. I looked up. It was Skinny, along with this chubby guy from up the street who was in the other fourth-grade class.

"I'm Andy. I just moved in," Skinny said. "So, who's gonna win the World Series?"

I scrunched my nose. "How should I know?"

The kid from up the street snickered.

"Marty here says your name is Mohammed." Andy grinned. "That's, like, the Prophet, right? So, if you're the Prophet, who's gonna win the World Series?"

I looked from Andy to Marty and back again. "Hunh?"

"It's a joke, dummy," Andy sighed. "So is your name really Mohammed?"

"Yeah," I said. "Is your name really Andy?"

Marty looked at me like I was mental. But Andy laughed. When Marty saw Andy laugh, he laughed too.

Andy grabbed my hand and hoisted me to my feet. "You know that fence that runs along the back of our yards?" he whispered, an eye over his shoulder. "Well, there's a space at the bottom behind the bushes at the end of our garden. Me and Marty are gonna crawl under it, into the golf course. Wanna come?"

I knew I should ask Mom, but I didn't want to look like a wuss. Besides, she and Dad belonged to the club and were always complaining about kids trespassing. So if I asked, she'd say no for sure, and I'd be a snitch as well as a wuss—and never have any friends, ever.

I scratched my butt. "Okay."

Andy scouted for grownups, as we snuck onto the course and ran from tree to tree, crawling through the rough till we hit the dogleg on the tenth hole. There's a dip in the fairway, where you can't be seen from the tee-off. "Hey," Andy said, "let's wriggle out and grab the golfers' balls. We can toss 'em in the tall grass, and watch their faces."

This turned out not to be such a great idea, on account of Mrs. Bennett. She was standing up in her golf cart, watching Mr. Bennett's drive through her binoculars. I never knew old people could yell so loud. All of a sudden, there were golf carts everywhere, chasing us. We got away, but an hour later my parents got a call from the club manager. Being the only Iranian-looking kid on the course, I'd kind of stood out.

"I didn't touch any golf balls," I told my folks. "I just

checked a few to see which brands went farthest."

"You expect us to believe that?" Dad said. "Who were the others?"

"There weren't any others. I was on my own. I figured it was okay cuz we have a family membership."

Dad smacked his forehead. "Lies and more lies!" He went on a rant about how he and Mom had moved to Meadowvale before I was born, when the subdivision first opened up; how they'd had to threaten to go to court to get the developer to sell to them; but how we finally belong—"I'm on the club's planning committee! Your mother's in the Ladies' Invitational!"—only I'd turned into this juvenile delinquent.

"But I didn't do anything!" I gave Mom a Bambi look. She put her arm around me. "Mohammed's a good boy. If he said he didn't do anything, he didn't."

I felt like a total turdball. I mean, I'd never done anything bad before, at least not that I could remember. And I'd certainly never lied about it. Especially not to Mom.

Still, that night as I crawled under the covers, I couldn't help thinking about the fun I'd had with Andy and Marty, sneaking through the trees and bushes, pretending we were spies. They might be a little dangerous in the Getting Me Into Trouble Department. All the same, I couldn't wait to see them again.

I got my wish. Next morning I was back at the anthill when Marty screeched up to Andy's door on his bike. I waved, but he hardly nodded. It was like us being friends was a dream. But in a sec, Andy barreled out, and everything was fine again.

"Hey, Prophet," he hollered.

"Hey, Prophet," Marty echoed.

They ran over, Andy in the lead. I hopped to my feet.

"Marty's gonna bike me round the neighborhood," Andy said with a friendly punch to my shoulder. "You up for it?"

"Sure. I just have to ask—"

But Dad had already stepped out of the garage, a storm in his eye.

"This is my dad," I said cautiously. "Dad, these are my new friends, Andy and Marty. Andy's just moved in."

Dad nodded. "Welcome to the neighborhood."

"We're going biking," I said. "Okay?"

"Your mother and I need you inside." And he clapped his hands. I ran inside, humiliated. He sat me down at the kitchen table. Mom stood by the sink while he grilled me: "Why did those boys call you 'Prophet'?"

I played with the fringe of the tablecloth. "I don't know."

"Hands on the table," Dad said.

I put my hands on the placemat and rubbed my fingertips over the cotton weave.

"Now then," Dad repeated, "why did they call you 'Prophet'?"

"You know why," I mumbled.

"Yes, I know why. But I want you to say it."

I closed my eyes. "It's because of my name. Mohammed."

Dad sucked in air through his teeth.

"Dad, it's just a nickname."

"I know about nicknames," he said slowly. "'Prophet' is not *just* a nickname."

"Dad, it means they like me. . . . It means I'm their friend."

"You don't need friends like that."

Mom put a hand on his shoulder. "They didn't mean anything, Arman. They don't know any better, that's all. Mohammed will set them straight. Won't you, Hammed?"

My ears burned. "Yesterday, you were so proud about

fitting in," I said quietly. "Well, what about me?"

"Belonging isn't the same as fitting in," Dad replied. "Your mother and I have never compromised who we are. And we never will, Inshallah." He sat beside me and put his hands on mine. "If you don't respect the Prophet, Hammed, you don't respect who you are. And if you don't respect who you are, no one else will either." He paused. "Those boys. They were with you on the golf course, weren't they?"

I stared at the center of the place mat.

"Without trust there is nothing," Dad said quietly. "Don't ever lie to us again."

"I'm sorry."

He gave me a squeeze. Mom kissed the top of my head.

Later, I went over to Andy's. Marty was already there. The two of them were watching Mr. J. mount the basketball backboard on their garage. I told them what Dad said.

"So what are we supposed to call you, then?" Andy asked.

"How about my name?" I said. "Mohammed. Or Hammed for short."

Marty looked puzzled. "Don't you have another one?"

"What's wrong with Mohammed?"

"Nothing. It's just kind of . . . you know . . ."

I wanted to say how there's baseball players called Jésus. And what about all the Matthew, Mark, Luke, and Johns? Or the Mary and Josephs? The Jacob, Isaac, Rachel, and Sarahs, for that matter? But I didn't. "My middle name's Sami."

Andy brightened. "Sammy. Like Uncle Sam. Great."

Actually, no—like plain Persian "Sami," I thought. But I didn't say anything. Andy seemed happy, and I didn't want to confuse him. Or maybe I just didn't want to sound weird or get asked any more questions.

Dad wasn't so pleased about my name change, but Mom cooled him down. "Give the boy a break, Arman," she said. "Sami's his middle name. Your father's name. How can you argue with that?"

Sami/Sammy. The day my name changed is the first time I realized that The Truth and The Whole Truth aren't necessarily the same. And how even a simple thing like a name can mean different things to different people.

Anyway, before Andy arrived, Mom used to drive me to school on her way to work at Pharmacy Value. Now I biked with my new buddies. It was a whole other world. I mean, Andy's a born Friend Magnet. I'd gone to Meadowvale Public since kindergarten, but on his first day there, he was the one making introductions. "You know Sammy?" he'd say on the playground. "He's my friend from next door."

Kids who'd ignored me as "Mohammed," the nut bar who sleeps at recess, paid attention to me as "Sammy," the guy with the cool friend who could think up stuff to do that'd freak their folks. Marty got new respect too; he wasn't just "the fat goof" anymore. It helped that Andy was a year-and-a-half older; he lost an early grade when his mom tried to homeschool him, and got distracted.

I'm not sure what Andy gets out of our friendship; I'm not sure he thinks about it. I just know that no matter how many other friends he's had, we're the ones he pals around with. The chosen ones. His biggest cheerleaders. His entourage.

It's been great. But right before graduating to Meadowvale Secondary, I had that thing with Mary Louise Prescott and her mother's little club, and Dad stuck me in the Theodore Roosevelt Academy for Boys, where I'm part of the class leper colony. I still hang with Andy and Marty when I can, and we text, and sometimes play video games online, but after a year it's not the same, us being at different schools and all.

I think about that as the three of us splash our feet in the park fountain opposite Mr. Softy's, and talk about the new year coming up—eleventh grade.

"We're gonna get Bonehead again. How'll we cope?" Andy groans to Marty—Mr. Boney being the math teacher who landed him in summer school. Andy and Marty have all their other teachers in common too, thanks to arranging identical schedules.

Marty pokes Andy in the ribs. "Bonehead has nothing on Calhoun." He imitates some teacher who apparently walks bow-legged, with his knuckles dragging on the ground.

Andy practically pees himself. "That's him! Remember last year when his foot got stuck in the wastebasket?" Whoops of laughter from the two of them. Me, I just sit there with a pasted-on smile. Who's Calhoun?

It's like I'm a ghost: I'm here, but they don't see me. They've moved on. I'm nothing but air. A wave of sickness washes over me. "I better go."

They look up, sort of surprised. "It's not even eight," Andy says.

"Dad." I roll my eyes. I feel bad using Dad as an excuse, but hey.

They drop me at home and take off. I watch the Deathmobile disappear around the corner for adventures unknown. Part of me wishes I was still with them; the other part of me knows if I was, I'd be feeling even worse.

Three

Mom passes me the chick-peas. "So, Sami, what are your three Events of the Day?"

Welcome to my family's dining room, a.k.a. The Interrogation Chamber.

The Johnsons eat in front of various TVs, depending on who's watching what. The Pratts eat together in their kitchen. What a zoo! Marty, his parents, three younger sisters, widowed grandma, and her aging rat-dog Mister Bubbles, everyone elbows up, yakking, sticking their forks into each other's food, while Mrs. Pratt frisbees fresh platters off the stove, and Mr. Bubbles hops onto laps to lick noses and beg scraps. Honest, the Pratts could charge admission.

We Sabiris, on the other hand, are "Civilized." That means we sit at the dining room table, Mom and Dad at either end, with china plates, linen napkins, butter knives, and candles, and discuss the Events Of The Day, meaning three things that've happened to us since breakfast. Dad says this builds families. I say it sucks my brains out.

The three Events Of The Day ritual started my first day back to school. Now, three weeks into the term, every day is same-old-same-old, and what used to be an Event is so old it ought to be buried. I mean, the only Event in my life worth mentioning happens tomorrow: my trip to Toronto with Dad. But okay, if Mom wants to drive me Skippy, I may as well have some fun.

"My three Events Of The Day." I pause, scoop chick-peas onto my plate, and pass the bowl to Dad. "Event Number One." I swivel the serving spoon through the rice dish, catching as many raisins as I can. "Today in the caf, three juniors barfed the lasagna special."

Mom closes her eyes. "Sami, please, we're eating."

"So were *we*."

"I thought we agreed our events would be positive."

"This *is* positive. Last year, guys were hurling on day one."

Mom looks to Dad for reinforcement. "Arman?"

Dad grunts absently, lost in his chick-peas.

I decide not to press my luck. "Okay, something *positive*. As of period three, I'm no longer the biggest nerd in school. The title's gone to Mitchell Kennedy."

"Ah, Mitchell." Mom brightens. "The friend from your noontime study group."

"Mitchell's hardly my friend. And we're hardly a study group. More like the Loser Lunch Bunch. Anyway, Mitchell's already read our entire science textbook. And today he told Mr. Carson. In class. It went over *real* well."

"Maybe he shouldn't have bragged," Mom says. "But it never hurts to work hard. You should invite Mitchell over sometime."

"Why?"

Mom sighs. "So don't." She offers me the tray of pistachio chicken. "And event number three?"

I take a breast. "Mr. Bernstein's had a miracle."

"Mr. Bernstein. Your history teacher, right? The older gentleman we met at the Academy open house?"

"Right." I hold the tray for her. "Mr. Bernstein's hair has been gray since forever. But overnight it magically turned black."

Mom laughs. "I like Mr. Bernstein." She takes a thigh. "He's so gracious. So fit. So stylish. He has a lucky wife."

A wife? Mr. Bernstein? Yo, Mom, get with the program. I set the tray beside Dad.

"Your turn, Arman," Mom says. "What's new in the world of microbes?"

Dad looks up from his chick-peas, frowns, takes a chicken leg, and places it in a nest of rice. "Well . . ." He pours orange gravy over it. "Well . . ." He carves a bite, sticks it in his mouth, chews slowly, swallows, and pats his lips with his napkin. "Well . . ."

"Yes," Mom says, "we've heard that bit."

Dad sets his napkin aside and plants his hands on either side of his plate, "All right. Here it is. About tomorrow, Sami. Our weekend. My colleague, Auggie Brandt, was scheduled to speak at the Saturday night dinner. But he's sick. He's asked me to fill in."

"You told him no, of course," Mom says.

"I wanted to. But Auggie's done me a lot of favors. So . . ."

"There is no 'So,'" Mom's eyes narrow. "Saturday, you're taking Sami to a doubleheader. The two of us discussed this. We planned it. We agreed it was important."

"I know. And it is," Dad says. "But I can't." He turns to

me. "Sami, I'm sorry."

I shrug. "There's still the Leafs game tomorrow night. And Saturday I can go to the ball games on my own."

Dad shakes his head. "Not possible. Tomorrow night I'll be preparing. And I don't want you out alone in a strange city. We'll do our getaway some other time."

"You mean the whole weekend is canceled?"

He opens his palms, like it's out of his hands.

The bottom drops out of my stomach. "No, Dad, please! I've told everyone. Besides, it's Canada. Nothing bad ever happens in Canada. It's safer than day care."

"I have a solution," Mom interrupts. "I'll call Deb right now, trade my shifts at the pharmacy, and come along. It'll be a family trip." She gives me a nod. "While your father works, I'll take you to the games."

"But you hate sports," I say.

"This weekend will be an exception."

Dad's face clouds. "It's a nice idea, Neda, but not practical."

"Who cares about practical?"

"Not in front of Sami," Dad signals.

"Arman," Mom says evenly, "if you can't accompany Sami, I will."

"Impossible. I'll be working. I'll need to concentrate."

"Then Sami and I will stay in a separate room."

"Out of the question."

"What do you mean, 'out of the question'?"

I wish I was ten so I could slide under the table.

"I mean it's too late," Dad says. "I've released the tickets."

"You've what?" Mom rocks back in her chair. "Without talking to me?"

"There wasn't time."

"There's always time. A simple phone call."

"I wasn't thinking."

"It's okay, Mom," I say.

"No," she whispers. "It's not."

"I'll make it up to both of you, Inshallah," Dad says. "The first free weekend I have, we'll all go to New York. How's that? Neda, you can do some shopping. Sami, I'll get us tickets to the Yankees. What do you say?"

I turn to Mom. "May I be excused?"

She nods. We both get up.

Dad's stunned. "Neda?"

But Mom's already halfway to the family room. It's the first time she's left a meal with dishes on the table. I hear the French doors close, the sound of the TV. I grab my plate and head to the kitchen.

"I said, I'll take us to New York!" Dad pleads.

"Yeah, right, whatever."

"Sami . . ."

I spin around. "Look, Dad, just forget it, okay? It's no big deal. You obviously have way more important things to think about than me."

Four

Holy shit. What just happened? Mom and Dad—
they never fight, aside from private discussions
in their bedroom. Plus Dad didn't order me back when I
stormed out. Is there a full moon or something?

I go to scrape my meal into the pail under the sink,
but the pistachio chicken still looks tempting. I bring my
plate downstairs to my bedroom—which I'm officially
renaming the Asshole Relief Center, in honor of Dad—
and slip behind my computer.

Andy and Marty are already online. I fill them in about
Dad and the weekend.

ANDY: tht sux!

ME: u sed it. mayb we can get 2gethr insted?
ANDY: cant. were off 2 my cottage.

They're going to the cottage without me *again*? I want to heave all over the keyboard.

ME: y dnt u tl me???
MARTY: u wr bzy.
ANDY: its not 2 l8. can u come?

My heart somersaults.

ME: w8 1 sec.

I race upstairs. Mom's left the family room for the kitchen, where she's putting Saran Wrap over the leftovers.

"Where's Dad?"

"Up in his office," she says briskly. "He got a call. Don't bother him."

No kidding. I made that mistake last week. The door was closed. He was on his cell. I tapped to see if it was okay for me to have a swim at Andy's. He went ballistic: "How long have you been listening in? What did you hear?"

You'd think I'd hacked into the Pentagon or something.

Mom sees me fretting. "What's so important you can't ask your mother?"

I spill the invitation.

"That's wonderful," Mom says. "Of course you can go."

"Thanks. But shouldn't we check with Dad?"

She takes me by the shoulders. "Sami, I've given permission."

Right. And I'm not going to blow it. In a flash, I'm back at the computer: IM IN!!!!!

Andy types the drill for our trip.

I'll get picked up after class for the drive to Alexandria Bay, where the Johnsons moor their boat. I'll have my passport and a note from Mom, but going over the border by water is a snap. The Js have a pass. They're supposed to notify authorities before a trip if they have guests, and phone from a landline on arrival. They never do. On paper, there's penalties, but nobody hassles cottagers.

Andy's fingers explode typos: "btw" has become "blt." We switch to webcams.

"So. Very important," Andy rattles. "Bring rubber boots, flashlights, hoodies, sweaters, and windbreakers. It's cold on the water."

"Check, check, check, and double-check," I say.

Andy grins so wide I'm surprised his head doesn't split in two. "Wait'll you see the abandoned hermit's shack we found. It's a couple of miles from the cottage, on an island the size of your thumb."

"What's this about a hermit?"

"Okay, maybe there isn't a hermit," Marty corrects. "But if there isn't one, there should be. The shack's made out of rotted plywood, it's caved in, and there's garbage all around, like rusty oil bins and bicycles and smashed-up TVs. We pictured this wacked-out hermit dropping dead under a full moon, and wild animals eating his bones."

"Not so loud!" Andy hisses. He switches off his overhead light, like that'll make things quieter. "The thing is," he whispers, "Hermit Island's covered in pines. From the water, that's all you see, plus a half-sunk dock. We stumbled onto it by accident. Key point: The island's got a small beach, great for goofing off. It's our own party central."

"One rule, Sammy," Marty interrupts. "No pouring your beer in the sand."

"Ha ha." When I'm with the guys at house parties, I carry a beer as a prop, so people won't think I'm a freak. Throughout the night I pour it down the toilet on pee breaks.

"Focus, team!" Andy says, eyes twitching. "Remember to bring sleeping bags. No, never mind, there's extras at the cottage. And a tent."

"We're going to camp there?" I exclaim.

"Duh. Yeah."

"With your dad?"

"You kidding?" Andy leans into his webcam; his left eyeball fills the frame. "Dad hates camping."

"Won't he mind us taking the boat overnight?"

The Eyeball winks. "No way. We're in eleventh grade now. Plus I've turned seventeen, remember? I'm telling you, man, it's gonna be cool. Way cooler than the cottage. And best of all, no neighbors to get pissed if we're out late making noise." Andy rolls his chair back. "We'll fish off the tires by what's left of the dock, get drunk—at least Marty and I will—and it'll be great. Sammy, you can be the designated pilot."

"You mean it? Me? Behind the wheel?"

"You bet. I'll teach you how to steer. Nothing to it. But, hey, Hermit Island is secret. No telling anyone, right?"

"Right!" I fake knuckle the screen, and laugh.

Hermit Island! Piloting a boat! I can't wait.

* * *

31

And now I can't sleep.

It's three A.M. I'm going out of my mind. I'm excited about Andy's cottage. But I'm scared about Dad. My folks always talk things over before I get permission for anything. This time Mom's gone solo. What if Dad finds out?

Well, what if he does? It's not like Mom and I are being sneaky, is it? I mean, she didn't tell me *not* to tell him, did she? And if it's important for him to know, she'll tell him herself, right? Who am I kidding? After their fight?

Anyway, how would he find out? I'll be back Sunday; he's gone till Monday. And if he calls, Mom can say I'm out or in bed. Still . . .

Maybe I should tell him before he leaves. No, it's too late. He'd say we snuck behind his back. I'd have snitched on Mom, and my permission would be canceled on the spot. Especially given the vibes since supper. Like, evening prayers were from the Land of Get Me Out Of Here! None of us looked at each other. We didn't even say good night after.

I hear someone in the kitchen. It's Dad. He's pacing in circles, top of the stairs, murmuring from the Qur'an, verses about peace, justice, and mercy. I know because I left my room door open, so I could hear if he and Mom got into it in the middle of the night. The cupboard door opens, closes. Now the fridge. Now the cutlery drawer. He'll be mixing a spoonful of molasses into a glass of milk.

I leave my room and crouch in the dark basement hall at the foot of the stairs. I hear Dad place a kitchen chair back from the table to sit—he never drags the chairs, says that could scratch the tiles. I hear the spoon rattle against the glass as he stirs, hear it clink on the small saucer where he always sets it. And now I hear a low groan, and the sound of Dad struggling to control his breath.

I go up the stairs, stop in the doorway. "Dad?"

He sits bolt upright. "Sami?"

"I got up to pee. Thought I heard something."

He tries to smile. "Just me and my milk and molasses. You should get back to bed."

"Can't sleep."

"That makes two of us."

I stand there, not knowing what to do. Then I edge over to the table and slip onto the chair opposite him. His eyes are red.

Dad catches me staring. "What are you looking at?"

"Nothing." I glance at the calendar on the side of the fridge, embarrassed.

Silence.

I try to think of something to say. I can't. Dad can't either. So we don't say anything. Just sit there, very still, for what seems like forever.

Finally, Dad says, "About our weekend . . . Are you okay?"

I shrug. "We can see the Yankees some other time."

"Good." He clears his throat. "Maybe you and your friends can get together, Inshallah. Do something fun."

I shrink a bit. "Sure. Maybe."

Dad reaches across the table. He grips my hand. "Sami . . ." His throat's so dry the words barely choke from his lips. "Sami, there's things I can't talk about. Things I can't explain. Understand?"

"I guess."

"Good." Dad gives my hand an extra squeeze. His knuckles are white. "Now go back to bed. Get some sleep."

I turn at the railing. Dad's staring after me with this haunted look. I want to say, "I love you," but I can't. He gives me his fake smile and his tight little wave.

I disappear into the dark.

Five

Dad's gone when I get up.

Mom and I do morning prayers, then have a quick breakfast of scrambled eggs and toast. It's as if last night never happened. But it did.

"Mom," I say, "about the fight . . . about the cottage . . ."

She raises her hand. "What's done is done."

"Maybe I shouldn't go."

"Don't be silly." She takes a no-nonsense sip of coffee. "You were promised a trip, and you're getting a trip. The cottage is a great chance to be with your friends. And the Johnsons are good parents; you'll be well-supervised, Mashallah."

I doodle a piece of egg with my fork. "So what do we tell Dad?"

A slow sip. Pause. "About what?"

"You know what. The cottage."

"Why say anything?" Mom says carefully. She spreads her toast with raspberry jam. "Do you tell your father every time you blow your nose?"

"This is bigger than that."

Mom bites into her toast, as if I haven't said a thing.

"He'll find out, Mom."

"How, unless you tell him?"

"I don't know. But what if he does? Not telling will make it worse."

Mom chews slowly, fussing the odd raspberry seed with her tongue. She dabs her lips with her napkin. Then she strokes my hair above the ear. "Sami," she says, "last night I acted in haste and anger. That was wrong. But why toss a match in a dry field? If your father finds out about the cottage, I'll handle it. Till then, let him stay a happy man, Inshallah. Agreed?"

I nod, but I'm not so sure.

We clear the dishes and get dressed. Dad said I'd get used to wearing the Academy uniform: navy blazer with school crest on the breast pocket, gray pleated flannels, and red tie. Who was he kidding? The blazer's stiff, the flannels itch, and the jocks think that choking me with my tie is major entertainment.

I bring my duffel bag and backpack to Mom's car, the duffel crammed with stuff for the cottage, the backpack with school books. Mom's driving me to the Academy on her way to work; cycling with everything would be crazy. Usually she's quick out the door, but not today. If she doesn't get a move on, we'll be late and I'll be on Vice Principal McGregor's radar; there's nothing he likes more than giving detentions.

I check my watch. It feels weird hanging around for a ride, like when I was little. But it feels even weirder when Mom steps out the door.

She's wearing her head scarf! Her green silk hijab! She never wears it in public except at mosque. Why now? I don't have to ask. It's about Dad and last night and the weekend. As we drive down our street, I slide lower and lower in my seat.

Mom reads my mind like I read hers. "Sami, it's just a scarf."

"Tell that to the guys. They don't understand head covering."

"Right," she says. "In their caps and hoodies."

We turn out of our neighborhood onto Oxford Drive. Ride past Meadowvale Plaza, construction, box stores, make a left onto Valley Park Road.

I see Academy Hill in the distance. *Allah, God, kill me now.*

"Please, Mom. Take it off before we get there?"

"I can't, Sami," she says. "Not today."

"Then let me out. I'll walk from here."

"What?"

"Really, Mom. I get razzed enough. You don't know what it's like."

"Oh, don't I?"

But she pulls over. Puts on her flashers. Stares straight ahead as I grab my stuff from the back seat. It's like I'm an ax murderer.

"Mom," I say, "it's not my fault you feel guilty."

"And it's not my fault you're ashamed to be you."

"You sound like Dad."

"What if I do?"

Cars are backing up behind us. Somebody honks.

"We're holding up traffic," Mom says. She tries to smile. "Have a nice weekend." And she drives off.

I make my way to the Academy's front gate and head along Roosevelt Trail toward the school. Maybe it was a trail in the old days. Now it's a paved road lined by a trimmed boxwood hedge. An Olympic-sized track surrounds the football field on the left; the principal's residence, field house, and three baseball diamonds are on the right. I catch my breath at the foot of Academy Hill. At the top, a statue of Teddy Roosevelt on a charging horse stands guard between the Middle School and the Upper School. The horse has the biggest balls in the world. Last Halloween, somebody painted them bright blue. We laughed ourselves sick watching them get scrubbed. Vice Principal McGregor had this big assembly about how it wasn't funny. That made us laugh even more.

Despite the blue balls prank, the Academy has this rep as one of the best private boys' schools in upstate New York. When it started in the mid 1900s, there was nothing around but cows and country, and kids got shipped here for the term. Now it's surrounded by urban sprawl, and half of us are day boys. According to the brochure, it's got everything except girls. Which is exactly why Dad stuck me here. Thank you, Mary Louise Prescott.

Mary Louise sat across from me in eighth grade at Meadowvale Middle School. Her mother was the parent volunteer for this after-school group called Living with Joy; Mary Louise was secretary-treasurer. It was basically a Christian club with donuts, Coke, and tambourines.

Anyway, Mary Louise started smiling at me in class, and at lunch she had this magic way of always being around whenever Andy and Marty were distracted by some girl, which in Andy's case was practically always. Mary Louise wore puffy sweaters, and smelled of peaches and starch. I didn't mind. She shared her chocolate bars with me.

But that's not all she wanted to share. One day she gets me alone at the edge of the tarmac, all serious like somebody's died. She says she hasn't slept for weeks and really needs to talk to me.

I go, "Sure."

And she takes a deep breath and says, "Sammy, I have to tell you about Jesus."

"I already know about him." I shrug. "He's one of our prophets."

"No!" She shakes her head. "He's not just a prophet. He's the Savior."

I'm like, "Okay. Fine. Want some gum?"

"I mean it, Sammy. You have to believe. How can I be happy up in Heaven if you're burning in Hell?"

Needless to say, I tried to avoid her after that. Only Andy told me I was crazy, that she was really into me, and he'd heard stories, and I should go for it. I'd never had a girl after me before—or since—so I'm thinking, hey, maybe he's right. And next time I bike by her place and she waves me over, I stop.

"Want to come in for some Ben and Jerry's? Meet my mom?" she asks.

The mom part freaks me out, but I'm up for the ice cream. Only Mary Louise takes me in through the attached garage. Before she opens the side door, she turns to me. "Sammy," she says, "would you like to touch my boobs?"

"What?"

"If you promise to come to the Living with Joy Club, you can touch my boobs."

"Isn't that against the rules or something?"

"Nothing's a sin if you have a pure heart and do it for Jesus," she says.

Next thing I know, my hand's up her sweater groping her bra, she's speaking in tongues, and I've developed this Seriously Big Problem. Which is exactly when Mrs. Prescott opened the garage door and caught us.

Well! Mrs. Prescott made Mary Louise confess her sin to the Living with Joy Club. Mary Louise cried, and everyone said a prayer, and apparently God forgave her.

I, on the other hand, was some heathen sex pervert. For months, any girl seen within a mile of me lost her reputation on the spot. Andy and Marty thought it was stupid; I hadn't even touched skin. But the rumors were way more exciting than the truth, so they're what people believed.

My parents included. Mrs. Prescott called them immediately after chasing me down her driveway with a rake. According to her, it was only a matter of time before I'd end up in a juvenile psych ward. I got sat down at the kitchen table and screamed at for what seemed like forever. The same old blah, blah, blah about how I'd shamed the family, ruined our good name, and made it hard for Mom and Dad to show their faces in the neighborhood.

I thought I'd get off the hook by telling Dad that Mary Louise had tried to convert me. It just made him madder: "How dare that school have a club for religious recruitment? And how dare you try to use that to shirk your responsibility? You know what the Prophet says about fornicators!"

Excuse me? I touched a bra. On invitation. You'd think Dad was Mrs. Prescott.

Mom tried to remind Dad about "the challenges

of puberty," but he went on this rant about Girls and Temptation, and how I needed to learn Discipline and spend less time with Bad Influences—meaning Andy and Marty, only he couldn't mention them by name because they're neighbors, and he had no intention of moving.

Long story short, I got stuck at this dump, a school supposedly free of Distractions, i.e., girls, that lead to Impure Thoughts That Defile the Soul.

The clock tower blasts "Reveille." Five minutes to homeroom. Then English, Math, lunch, Science, History, and finally the bell—freedom.

I bust my ass up Academy Hill. And into Academy hell.

Six

Last period. History. Cottage countdown.

Mr. Bernstein's at the front of the class, trimmed and gelled, in a cream suit and a yellow-striped tie. As per usual, he starts with a short lecture full of personal opinions guaranteed to get us talking. Sometimes he gets heat from parents for straying off the course curriculum or saying stuff that's controversial, but he doesn't care. "I've taught here since the dinosaurs," he jokes. "You're stuck with me."

Today he's riffing on witch hunts in colonial Salem and medieval Europe. "Terrifying times for anyone different," he exclaims with a sweep of his hand. "Leaders traded in fear. People spied on each other. And rumors got people burned at the stake." Mr. Bernstein's pretty entertaining, especially when his arms get going, but there's forty-three minutes to go, and I couldn't care less.

I look over at Mitchell Kennedy. His lips are moving. Mitchell repeats everything teachers say as soon as they say it. He says it helps him remember things. Whatever.

Forty-two minutes to go. Fridays, Andy and Marty have a last period spare, so Mr. J should have them here waiting for me by the bell. I close my eyes, imagine the smell of fish and pine, the sight of rock crags breaking water.

Forty-one minutes, thirty seconds to go. I count the holes in the ceiling's acoustic tiles. I look at the poster of George Washington; I think about his wooden teeth. He kissed with those things. Did he brush them? Sand them? Did he ever get dry rot?

Forty-one minutes, twenty seconds to go. Why does time take forever?

Ow.

Eddy Harrison's jabbed me in the back with his pen. Full name: Edward Thomas Harrison the Third. Yeah, The Third. That's why I've nicknamed him Eddy Duh Turd. He's on the football team and is majorly huge from doing weights. Not to mention steroids. The 'roids have bulked him up, but they haven't helped his acne any. His zits are big as cauliflowers. He could enter them in a contest, win a prize or something.

Eddy waits a minute and jabs me again. Dad says, "Bullies want a reaction. Ignore them and they'll stop." Dad's stupid advice has nothing to do with bullies. It's about keeping me out of fights, which would get me into trouble, which would hurt his precious reputation. As in, "What you do reflects on this family." Meaning him.

Eddy jabs me a third time.

I turn in my seat. "Quit it," I whisper.

"Or what?" Eddy grins. Even his teeth have muscles.

Mr. Bernstein claps his hands. "Harrison? Sabiri?"

"Sorry," I say. "Just stretching."

Mr. Bernstein gives us The Look, then rears back his head and goes on about witch trials. "The accused could be tortured into confession. Evidence could be secret or based on hearsay. After all," he tilts his eyebrows, "if the accused is guilty, who needs a fair trial?"

Dave Kincaid, in the far aisle, throws up his arm. "But what about their rights?"

"They didn't have any," Mr. Bernstein says. "And that's an important point, Kincaid. Thank you for raising it. We take our civil rights for granted. We shouldn't. They're something our ancestors fought for."

Eddy pushes the seat of my chair with his toe.

"Name the civil rights we cherish most," Mr. Bernstein challenges. He faces the blackboard, and scribbles down everything the class calls out: The right to free speech. Equality. Religion. Privacy. Assembly. A fair trial.

Eddy leans into my ear. He stinks of salami. "You told Bernstein you and Daddy would be in Toronto today. Wuzzup? Your camel run out of gas?"

I try not to hear. Try to copy the notes from the board.

"You deaf, Sabiri? Hunh?"

My hand shakes.

"Yo, sand monkey."

I whirl around. "Go screw yourself!"

Oh my god. Please tell me I didn't just yell "Go screw yourself." But I did. I can tell by the silence. The look on Mitchell's face. And the clear, cold sound of Mr. Bernstein's voice: "What did you say?"

I turn to Mr. Bernstein, prepared to die. But he's not staring at me. He's staring at Eddy. "Harrison, I'm talking to you. What did you call Sabiri?"

"Nothin'."

"Think hard."

Eddy taps his pen. "Who cares what I said? He swore at my mother."

"What a cowardly lie!" Mr. Bernstein's eyes burn. "Racism has no place in this class, Harrison. Report to Vice Principal McGregor."

Eddy gets up slowly, collects his books and backpack, and slouches up the aisle. "So much for freedom of speech." He stops at the door and pulls out his cell. By the time he hits the office, he'll have called his father with a story.

Mr. Bernstein doesn't care. "Where were we? Ah yes, rights. Spend the rest of the period organizing an essay on the civil right you value most, and the reasons you value it."

I try to work, but I can't. Eddy's steamed. He'll be after me. What'll I do?

I don't have to wonder long. Within minutes, he strolls back into the room with a smirk on his face. He hands Mr. Bernstein a readmit note.

Mr. Bernstein drops it in the wastebasket. "Your assignment's on the board." He watches Eddy like a hawk.

Eddy acts like he couldn't care less. He saunters down the aisle with a wave to his buddies, "accidentally" bumping into my desk before sitting down. Mr. Bernstein clears his throat.

"Sorry," Eddy says, all sarcastic.

Eight minutes to go. How will I escape?

The head secretary's voice comes over the PA: "Mr. Bernstein?"

"Yes?"

"Could you please send Sabiri to the office? Mr. McGregor would like a word with him."

Mr. Bernstein frowns. "Certainly."

Eddy leans in to my ear. "Thanks for getting me in shit. I'll be here, when you come for your books. You, me, and my boys, we'll have a little 'talk' in back of the field house."

Mr. Bernstein's eyes flicker, like he's heard. "You can take your things with you, Sabiri," he says casually.

Thank you, thank you. I get my knapsack from under my chair. I try not to sweat as I walk up the aisle, Eddy giving me the Evil Eye the whole way. I exit into the corridor. The office is to the left. I turn to the right. No way am I getting killed. Not now, before the weekend.

I run upstairs to my locker. Grab my duffel bag. Race down the hall to the far end, trip down the stairs, charge through the side door.

I loop around the building, turn at the statue, and cross the circular driveway onto Roosevelt Trail.

"Sabiri!"

It's Vice Principal McGregor. He's on the front steps. He must have seen me through the office window.

"Sabiri! Stop!"

I keep running.

"Sabiri! I said, 'Stop!'"

But I can't. I'm in too much trouble already.

I see the Johnsons' Camry speeding up Roosevelt Trail. Andy's at the wheel, Marty beside him. We pass each other. Andy squeals the brakes, pulls a one eighty, and catches up to me in a flash.

I jump into the back seat.

"What the hell?" Andy says.

"Drive!"

Seven

We're a mile down Valley Park Road before I catch my breath enough to tell Andy and Marty what happened.

Andy whistles. "What's your dad gonna do when he finds out you blew off a trip to the V.P.?"

"Don't ask. Between Eddy, McGregor, and Dad, I am dead, deader, deadest. So could we please not talk about it? I want a weekend to breathe before I die, okay?"

I pull jeans and a Sabres hoodie from my duffel bag, and change out of my Academy uniform as we cruise toward Inner Loop East and the New York State Thruway. Then it hits me. Somebody's missing.

"Uh, Andy," I say, "where's your dad?"

"Can't hear you." He laughs. "Music's too loud." Marty finds this majorly funny.

"No, really. Is he already at the cottage? Will he boat over to pick us up?"

Marty turns around in his seat and mouths, "What?" like we're in front of speakers at a rock concert.

I reach between the front seats and yank Andy's iPod out of its dock. "Cut it out. Why isn't your dad here?"

Andy squinches his nose. "Why should he be?"

"On the webcam, you said he hates camping, but he'd let us take the boat to Hermit Island. I thought that meant he'd be coming."

"Assume nothing," Marty says in this robot voice. "Your ways are not our ways, Earthling."

"Stuff the kiddie crap, Marty. What's up?"

"My folks are gone all week," Andy grins. "We'll be at the cottage on our own."

My eyes pop. "Do they know?"

"I didn't tell them, if that's what you mean." He winks into the rearview. "The way I figure, if they think I'm at home, they'll relax. It's my contribution to their trip."

"What if they try to reach you?"

"They'll call my cell. I'll be like, 'Oh, I'm so bored in

Meadowvale.' Meanwhile, I'll be cracking a cold one on the beach."

I look out the back window. Meadowvale's disappearing. I press my forehead against the upholstery and think about Mom. We were keeping this trip a secret from Dad. Now I'll be keeping a secret from her too. What if she finds out? I am *so* beyond worm meat.

Andy's free foot taps like Thumper. "It's no big deal, Sammy. A couple of times this summer, my folks left me and Marty alone for a day."

"Yeah, but not for the whole trip. And for sure not over to Canada solo."

"So what? I can pilot the boat, and we have our papers, which we won't even need."

"I told you he'd want to bail," Marty mutters.

My cheeks burn. "Who said anything about bailing? It's just, Mom thinks your parents will be there. That's how I got permission."

"So let her think that. How'll she find out anything different?" Marty asks.

"Come on," Andy coaxes. "It'll be fun. You'll get to make up for the summer."

"I guess." I say glumly.

Andy hunches over the wheel. "Don't wreck our

weekend, okay? If you wanna wimp out, I'll drive you back, drop you off at your place."

"Sure, we'll only have wasted half an hour," Marty crabs.

Andy slows down. "So what do you want me to do?"

I don't know I don't know I don't know I don't know.

"Fine," Andy sighs into the silence. "I'll take you home."

Marty slumps in his seat. "Waydego, Sabiri. You've turned into a real douchebag, you know that?"

My stomach heaves. After the past summer, this is it. My last chance. If I'm out today, I'm out forever. I won't see the guys again. Not as best friends anyway. I'll have nothing left but Academy hell.

I fake a laugh, bat Andy's headrest. "Okay, I'm in."

Andy brightens. "That's our Sammy!" He high-fives me over the back of his seat. "If there's a problem with your mom, blame me. Tell her you thought my folks were at the cottage till you arrived, and I wouldn't take you back. Yeah, that's it, say you were kidnapped!"

"Kidnapped to Canada. By space aliens," Marty adds in his robot voice.

"It's what would've happened too, if you hadn't gone and asked about my dad," Andy continues. "We tried to protect you, Sammy. Honest. But you wouldn't let us. You made us tell. Some things, it's better not to know."

I have a flash of Dad at the kitchen table, looking haunted. Hunted. *Sami, there's things I can't talk about. Things I can't explain.*

"Andy," I say, "turn up the music as loud as you can."

PART TWO

PART TWO

Eight

Thanks to Andy's heavy foot, we get to Alexandria Bay ahead of schedule. Still, it's six P.M.—only a couple hours of light left. We go to the drive-thru at McDonald's and stuff our faces with Quarter Pounders and fries on the way to the marina.

Outside the parking lot, kids are selling bait: earthworms in old Styrofoam containers scrounged from a local Chinese takeout joint. One container should do us, but Andy insists we get three.

The lot's almost full. Fathers and sons are getting back from a few hours' fishing, couples are heading out for a sunset cruise, and people like us are going to their cottages. Most everyone's white. I stay glued to Andy and

Marty, hands in my pockets, hoodie up, face down, trying my best to be invisible.

"What's with you?" Andy asks.

"Nothing. Just don't want to get hassled."

"Don't be so paranoid."

"Easy for you to say."

The Johnsons' boat is moored on Pier 4, Well 122. It's a Chris-Craft Catalina, twenty-three feet long, eight feet wide, with a deep-V hull. Mr. J wanted to call it *My Jolly Johnson*, but Mrs. J said that was crude. She wanted something lame like *Windsong* or *Serendipity*; in the end, she let him get away with *Cirrhosis of the River*.

We stash our duffel bags, knapsacks, and bait in the dry compartment of the bow. The Catalina rides waves well, so we shouldn't get wet unless Andy decides to set a speed record. Just in case, Marty and I zip nylon windbreakers over our hoodies.

I have to admit, Andy knows his stuff. His directions are crisp and clear. We loosen the ropes and cast off, slipping on life jackets from the storage bins under the rear seats.

Andy recognizes an old man down the pier and gives a wave. The man waves back.

I turn away. "Who's that?"

"Dunno. But I've been waving to him since I was six," Andy reassures. "Just chill, okay? Nobody gives a damn who we are or what we're doing. Look normal and you won't draw attention."

Right. For lots of guys like me, normal would be rolling out a prayer rug about now. Then watch that old man give us a friendly wave. He'd be waving for Homeland Security is more like it.

Andy steers us out of the marina to the St. Lawrence River. The breeze puffs up my windbreaker. I lean over the side of the boat and let the cold spray sting my cheeks. Somewhere out here in the water, there's an invisible east–west line: The border between us and Canada. Andy navigates through clusters of craggy rock islands dotted with trees and cottages.

"Are we in Canada yet?" I holler over the roar of the motor.

"Yeah," Andy hollers back.

So, I smile to myself, we've crossed the line without seeing it coming. I seem to be doing a lot of that lately.

Another twenty minutes and I spot Andy's cottage in a cove on the far mainland. Actually, it's more like a second home, winterized, with a car in the garage.

Other cottages dot the cove, each with fifty yards or

so of shoreline. Most are dark, some already boarded up for the winter, but a few have families out in sweaters enjoying barbecues, playing catch, tossing Frisbees, or throwing sticks in the water for their dogs to fetch.

Andy guides the Catalina in to his dock; it's lined with tires to cushion arrivals. All the same, Marty sticks the butt of an oar off the side to ensure a soft landing. We hop off and help Andy moor.

"It's almost sunset," I say. "Maybe we should go to Hermit Island tomorrow."

Andy bugs out: "We haven't come this far not to camp out!" He marches us into the kitchen, where we fill a cooler with junk food, plus frozen burgers and ice packs from the freezer. "You have your list for me, son?" he teases, in imitation of his dad.

"Shut up," I grin.

Every time I've gone to the Johnsons' cottage, Dad's given Mr. J a list of my prayer times, food restrictions, and movies I'm not supposed to watch. And each trip, Mr. J's nodded seriously and put the list in his pocket. "You'll remember all this stuff, won't you, Sammy?" Mr. J's asked me on the boat to the cottage. "Sure," I've said, and then forgotten about it. Back home, Dad always asks Mr. J if I've followed the rules, and Mr. J always says yes.

Dad never believes him. He grills me, especially about our meals. "Are you calling Mr. Johnson a liar?" I say. That shuts him up.

But why go nuts about that now? Dad isn't here to wreck things. I can relax.

We collect sleeping bags and air mattresses from the blanket boxes in the bedrooms and stash them in the Catalina's stern. Then we get the fishing rods from the umbrella stand by the side door and secure them in the fiberglass rod boxes. Andy checks the locked tackle box next to the console where Mr. J stores the flashlights. We have four, plus extra batteries.

Andy shifts from one foot to the other. "Hey, can the two of you finish up? There's something I gotta do." He runs inside.

Marty leads me to the woodbox near the compost heap, where we get the beer that he and Andy hid this summer, under a pile of kindling. Mr. J's let Andy drink since he turned fourteen, but Andy didn't want him to know they were boozing in the boat.

I fill the burlap sack with firewood.

Marty rolls his eyes. "We'll find loads of driftwood on the beach."

"What if it's too dark to see by the time we get there?"

"That's why we have flashlights."

"But what if it's wet? Like, what if it got rained on this week?"

"Fine," Marty grumps, "if you're gonna be a girl about it."

"This way's easy is all," I explain. "We can get our fire pit going right away without wearing down our batteries."

"I got it, Mom."

Our final trip is to the garage, where we rummage around for Andy's old tent. It's on a shelf, folded up inside a thick plastic sheet draped with cement dust, spider webs, and bits of dead leaves. It stinks of mildew.

"Whew!" I stick my nose to the side, as we carry it to the boat. "Marty, between this stench and your farts, we'll be dead by morning."

"Don't worry." He laughs proudly, "I brought matches."

"Great. We won't suffocate. We'll explode!"

We throw a tarp over everything in open storage and wait for Andy to finish whatever he's doing. I go sit at the end of the dock and dangle my legs over the side, watching the sun sink behind the cluster of islands to the southwest. Marty plunks himself down in back of the Catalina's engine. He bounces his chubby calves off the rubber tires along the side and starts to work out a splinter in his thumb, chewing at it with his teeth.

"So . . . ," he says, after what feels like forever.

"So."

He spits out the sliver. "Sammy . . ."

"Yeah?"

"Is there something I should know about?"

"Like what?"

"Are you pissed with me or something?"

"No," I lie. "Why?"

"Dunno. It's just, I've been getting this vibe." (*He's* been getting a vibe?) "So anyway, we're okay?"

"Yeah," I say. "Sure."

"Good." Pause. "Cuz you'd tell me if there was a problem, right?"

"Marty, quit it, will you?"

"But you would, right? Sometimes I do things, say things—I can piss people off. I don't mean to."

"I know."

Silence.

We listen to the boats in the water. Laughter from up the beach. A dog barking.

I look to the cottage. "I wonder what's keeping Andy?"

"Guess." Marty whispers it like I should know, but I don't. "He's been this way since he found out. Clowning around like nothing's the matter. Then bam. It hits him. He leaves class, holes up in the can till he's normal again."

What does Marty mean, *since he found out*? What does he mean, *normal again*?

Marty sighs. "He hides stuff pretty well."

Hides what? I'm dying to know, but I can't ask. If I do, Marty'll know that Andy hasn't told me. And why hasn't he, if we're best friends? My skin goes clammy. If I don't know Andy, who *do* I know?

"Yeah," I cover. "He hides stuff *real* well."

Marty scratches himself. "I'd be shaken up too, if I was him. Andy's always looked up to his dad. You know his mom's taking pills?"

"Sad," I say, like it's old news.

Andy bursts out of the cottage. "We're good to go."

Marty and I jump up. "Great!" But I'm thinking, *What's going on, pal? What's wrong with your parents?*

The sun's down. The sky's filled with a gray light, stray clouds lit from beneath in dull oranges, pinks, and purples.

Andy takes his place behind the wheel. Marty hops

aboard and takes the seat beside him, as the key turns in the ignition. I push off and take a seat behind.

"Hermit Island, here we come," Andy whoops.

"Aye, aye, Captain," Marty echoes.

We edge into the dark.

Nine

The guys make jokes as we skim through the water. I don't catch much over the noise of the engine, but I make sure to smile and give a thumbs-up whenever they turn around to see how I'm doing.

The breeze bites my skin. I huddle into myself, and watch the lights glimmering in the dark river air: Twinkles from roads and towns along the mainland, from cottages dotting the shore and ringing the maze of islands that swallow us up. Beams from boat lamps, too, navigating the channels: Sailboats, fishing boats, cabin cruisers, each with its own horn, its own bell, its own jumble of laughter, music, and engines.

I'm lost in the feel and the night of it. But Andy has

a map in his head from a lifetime of Thousand Island summers. "We're back in American waters," he says. Most of the cottages here are dark, boarded up. "These ones are owned by millionaires from the deep South who only come up for a week or two each summer to beat the heat."

We near a patch of tree-lined cliffs. Andy slows down and steers us between two walls of rock. We follow the wall on the right, then turn left and enter a stretch of water surrounded by five large islands. Andy cuts the engine. We drift forward with the current. It's quiet here, only the sound of distant echoes, and the light waves that lap against our boat and the islands' shores. Dark, too. No lights except our boat lamp, the stars, and the moon, which shimmer over the rippling water.

"This circle of islands belongs to the Stillman family," Andy says. "They're from Tennessee, I think. Each island has a master cottage, more like a mansion, with guest houses and outbuildings, all facing the outer river. A few years ago, old Mr. Stillman blew his brains out. His kids and grandkids have stayed away ever since."

I shiver. Is it the breeze?

Andy raises his arm and points. "There she is," he whispers. "Straight ahead, middle of the circle."

Hermit Island floats toward us out of the dark.

At first, it's hard to make out, dwarfed by the Stillmans' islands surrounding it. But as we near, I see the shape of a bank of pine trees a couple of hundred yards long. Nearer still, the boat lamp lights up a ghostly dock wobbling out from the shore, the rotten end collapsed into the water. There's a patch of sand to the right, with a large weathered sign:

PRIVATE PROPERTY! NO TRESPASSING!

"Are you sure it's okay to be here?" I ask.

"You mean the sign?" Andy chuckles. "Like anyone's around to care."

Which doesn't exactly answer my question.

Andy guides the boat to the dock. "Holler if you see Stillman's ghost," Marty jokes. "I picture bits of brain, maybe an eyeball, floating around what's left of his skull."

We moor the boat and haul our supplies over the wobbly dock to the beach. In a few minutes, our tent's set up, Andy and Marty have popped a few beers, and we're getting toasty round a campfire.

We're not the first partiers on this so-called deserted

island. The wind has blown some old beer cans and snack wrappers to the scruff behind the strip of beach. There's even a used condom hanging off some yellowed grasses. But we're the only campers here tonight.

Andy catches me staring up at the constellations. "Not bad, hunh?"

I smile. "Not bad."

"Little white lies," Marty winks. "They make the world go round."

It's so late the back of my eyes ache.

Andy and I are outside the tent, fully dressed, sitting on our sleeping bags. It was escape or die. The second Marty passed out, his gas attacks went into overdrive. Talk about global warming. His cheeks are flapping so hard his ass'll get windburn.

The campfire's low. I place a few logs on it. Andy's drunk, but he's sobered up some since throwing up. All the same, he keeps moaning about this girl from Meadowvale Secondary I've never met. This is the problem of me not drinking: If I was drunk, Andy wouldn't sound so stupid and boring.

"I should forget about Sarah," he says, staring into the embers. "Things never work out, anyway." I wonder if he's going to start telling me about his problems with his parents. Instead he says, "I should be a hermit."

"Yeah, right. Live happily ever after with your right hand."

"No, really," Andy says solemnly. "I'd find an island like this with a little hermit shack. I'd fish. Eat berries. Hunt squirrels." His head lolls. "You haven't seen the shack yet, have you?"

"No."

"Well, it's perfect. Perr. Fect. You should see it."

"I will," I say. "First thing tomorrow."

"No," he says, suddenly wide awake. "Now."

"It's too dark."

"We got flashlights." Andy waves his triumphantly and lurches to his feet.

"Great, we got flashlights," I stall. "But let's wait till morning. Marty'll want to go too."

Andy shakes his head. "Forget Marty. He's already seen it. I wanna go now."

"You're drunk."

"And you're a genius." He lets out a whoop and lopes haphazardly into the pines. "Race you to the shack."

"Andy, don't be crazy!"

His light dances away between the trees. I hear the

cracking of dead branches as he stumbles through the brush. The sounds disappear in the night.

I curl up in my sleeping bag, expecting him to come back any second. But he doesn't. What if he's tripped and cracked his head open on a rock? Or run across the island and fallen off a ledge, and now he's knocked out in the water, drowning? If I stay here and he dies, it'll be all my fault.

Damn, Andy.

I get my flashlight and follow him into the woods. It's not a big island, right? So it's not like I could get lost. Or run into a bear or a psycho hermit with a chainsaw. Well it's not—is it?

I've always been able to spook myself. Right now, I don't have to try. If I look straight up, I can see the odd star, but the light doesn't penetrate the woods. Here on the island floor, it's pitch black, except for the beam of my flashlight. It picks up fallen trees, roots stuck up into the air. Half the downed trunks are rotted, covered in a thick carpet of moss and pine needles.

I glimpse a creature off to the right. Swing my flashlight. Nothing. Just a weird shadow. Shadows everywhere.

I move slowly. The mulch hides crevasses in the rock. Surprises waiting to twist an ankle. Andy was insane to barrel in here.

"Andy?"

Silence.

I should see the light from his flashlight, but I don't. Not to worry—he's probably turned it off. I'll bet he's hiding behind some tree, waiting to jump out and scare me.

My foot catches on something. I stumble forward, trip face-first to the ground, my left leg snarled in a strip of barbed-wire fencing. The bottom of my jeans is ripped, but I'm okay. My flashlight picks up a row of old posts planted into the distance on either side of me. The fencing holds between some of the posts, falls away between others. Was it to keep things out? Or trap them inside?

I brush myself off. "Andy?" I sweep my flashlight back and forth. Ahead of me, a clearing. I toe my way forward, come out of the pines.

I'm at a garbage dump. It must be the one the guys talked about, next to the hermit shack. There's stacks of green plastic bags, and bundles of neatly tied magazines and newspapers, molting at the edges. I see a rusty baby carriage. Broken radios and TVs. Old Coca-Cola crates. And in the center of the junk, the shack itself, cobbled together from boards, plywood, and tarpaper.

"Andy?" I edge toward it. "Andy, I know you're hiding. Say something."

Nothing.

"Andy, this isn't funny."

The shack has a ripped screen door. It's fallen off its hinges, the frame peeling. I aim my flashlight into the black hole. I see Andy crouched in the corner of the shack, next to a couple of old paint cans.

"Gotcha!" I exclaim.

Andy doesn't budge. His eyes are huge. They're staring at something behind me.

"Andy?"

A beam of light hits my back, casting my shadow against the shack. "Drop your flashlight, boy," says a low voice. "Turn around slow, so I can see you."

I do as I'm told. Ahead of me, the hulking shape of a stranger. He's wearing a miner's helmet. I squint hard.

There's a twelve-gauge shotgun aimed at my head.

Ten

The man holding the shotgun is maybe sixty. He's wearing a dirty plaid jacket over dirtier overalls and boots. There's a hunting knife strapped to his belt. He hasn't shaved in days, or had a bath by the smell of him.

"You boys having fun?"

Alone at night on a deserted island with an armed psycho. Whaddaya think?

"Asked you a question," the hermit says. "You fancy this is some party place?"

"No, sir," I whisper.

"Damn right, it's not. There's a sign: NO TRESPASSING. Can't you read?"

"Sorry."

"'Sorry'? That's what they all say."

They? Who are *they*? Where are *they* now?

"You two alone?"

"Yes, sir."

"Don't lie to me, boy. There's a lard-ass passed out in your tent."

"I mean there's just the two of us, here, now," I cover. How long has he been spying on us?

"We just came to have fun," Andy blurts. "Please, let us go. We won't tell anyone you're here."

"You think I'm a fool?"

"I mean it. We won't tell anyone. And we'll never come back."

"For damn sure, you won't," the hermit spits. "On your feet."

He marches us through the woods, hands on our heads. Any second, he'll kill us and stuff our bodies in a rotten tree trunk. Who'll ever know? My folks always taught me to tell someone where I was going. This time I didn't. We didn't write anything down at the cottage, either. Stupid, stupid.

Marty's wailing from the beach: "Andy . . . Sammy . . . Where are you?"

We come through the pines onto the sand. Marty's

down by the water, taking a leak. He turns, dick in hand, sees the hermit, and falls on his ass.

"Toss me your knapsacks," the hermit says. "One at a time."

So he's going to rob us *before* he kills us. What if we rush him? No way. Andy and Marty are too drunk. If I go it alone, I'm done for sure.

The hermit crooks his rifle under his arm and kneels by our knapsacks. He fumbles out our passports, fishes a pad and pen from his jacket, and makes a few notes. Then he stands and faces us.

"You're on Stillman family property," he says. "I'm the Stillmans' caretaker. It used to be every few months punks like you'd come here to party. End-a this summer, twice a week. Well, fun's over. Sober up and clear out. If you're here past eight A.M., I call the Coast Guard and the New York State Police." He waves the shotgun. "Next time, I may not be so sociable. You're trespassers. Law'd be on my side. Understood?"

We nod.

"'Night, then." He disappears into the woods.

By dawn, we're packed and ready to go.

Andy's usually a fireball in the morning. Not today. He

sits on the dock, head down, like he's under a big DO NOT DISTURB sign. I'm collecting leftover beer cans and food wrappers. Marty's trying to douse the embers in our fire pit by sweeping sand over them with his foot.

"Caretaker, my ass," Marty grumbles. "That was no caretaker. What's a caretaker doing in a hermit shack?"

"Who says that's where he came from?" I say. "He could have seen our fire from a guest house on one of the other islands, and boated around behind us for surprise."

Marty sniffs. "I say he's a dirty hermit. Once we get back, we should report him."

"For what? Catching us trespassing?"

"Sure. Why should he get to use this island and not us?"

"Because he's got a gun, maybe?"

"And how's that right? Some nut with a gun terrorizing innocent campers?" Marty takes a break, hands on his knees. "I say we call the cops. Leave an anonymous tip."

"You think he won't figure out who sent it? He's got our names and addresses."

Marty shoots me a look. "You're a coward."

"Me?" I laugh. "You sure shriveled up good when we came out of the woods."

"You stared at my dick?"

"Not sure. It looked kind of small for a dick. Even yours."

Marty kicks sand at me.

I dance circles around him. "I saw a snail, maybe? A mosquito bite?"

"Yo." It's Andy, roused and ready to go. Marty grouches to the boat. I follow.

The ride to the cottage is quiet. Andy takes it slow, his skin as gray as the sky. Marty nods off beside him. I think about strangers in strange places, about what happened last night, and about what could have happened.

Once we land, we put the fishing rods back in the umbrella stand, the extra food in the freezer, and the cooler and tent in the garage. Marty and I go to bring in the sleeping bags, but Andy lingers behind by the old Chevy, the dinosaur his folks drive to town for food or a movie. I let Marty go ahead, and watch as Andy slumps onto the hump in the middle of the back seat, all six feet of him. His body's folded up like an accordion, head buried in his hands.

"Andy?" I say quietly.

He looks up, bewildered to see me. His face is completely hopeless, his eyelids rimmed a dull red.

"I used to be able to stand up in here," he says simply.

"I remember Dad driving, Mom in the passenger seat, and me looking out the window at cows, wondering what the cows were thinking, and rolling up the windows to keep out the dust blowing up from the dirt roads. Dad would put his hand on Mom's knee, and when we'd get back to the cottage, they'd say they were having a nap, and I'd wander up the beach collecting pebbles, investigating dead seagulls. Nothing lasts." He looks away. "Marty told you about my folks?"

"Sort of. Not really."

"I was wasted, or I wouldn't have told him. He's got a big mouth." He forces a smile. "It's okay you knowing though. Just don't tell anyone else, okay?"

"I promise."

Andy sucks in a breath. "My folks aren't on a trip. They're away for couples therapy. As if that'll work." His breath catches. "At first, I was mad at Mom for spying on him. Why did she have to check his cell phone records? Or hire a private detective? If there was a problem, why couldn't she pretend? Why couldn't we just go on?"

"Andy." I hesitate. "If it's a breakup, they happen. You'll get over it."

"No," he shakes his head. "This is worse. First week of school, I heard her howling. She had the doctor's report.

My dad—my perfect dad—he gave her an STI." Andy squeezes himself around the middle. "He got infected at the Paradise Club in Buffalo. Didn't know which ho gave it to him." He starts to rock.

"Andy . . ." I want to hold him, but I don't know how.

"I'm not sure what's going to happen," he says. "Or where home's going to be. Or what anything's going to be. I don't even know my dad. I mean, who is he?"

Marty's struggling up to the garage with the three sleeping bags and air mattresses. "Thanks for the help." I raise a hand. He sees what's up and puts everything down. We stay real still.

Andy wipes his eyes with his sleeve. He gets his legs out the door but stays hunched on the end of the seat. "Guys," he says, "mind if we just go home?"

Fast as a daydream, we're back at the marina. Seeing as we've been in Canada, we should check in with immigration. But like Andy says, "Why bother? As far as anyone knows, we never left home."

We drive into the country—no talking, just music. Andy taps the steering wheel like he's a drummer, while Marty plays air guitar in the passenger seat. I stretch out in back and pretend to sleep. What I really do is think about Andy's dad. And my dad.

I imagine Dad at security conferences. What does he do in those cities late at night, out of sight, away from home? I think about this weekend in Toronto. Why couldn't I go to the games on my own? I'll be sixteen in a few months, after all. And why couldn't Mom come? Why the big deal?

I go numb: Is Dad like Andy's dad? Is he cheating with someone? Is that why Mom was so mad? Has she guessed?

I picture Dad slinking into a bar, finding a seat in a dark corner, and slipping off his wedding ring. Or calling an escort service from his room. Or maybe the woman is somebody at the conference. Has he seen her before? Are these meetings a cover for them to hook up? Does she have a husband? A kid like me?

Stop. This is crazy. Dad's so righteous, if he ever had a wet dream he'd never sleep again; he'd staple his eyelids to his forehead. I mean, for him, me touching Mary Louise Prescott's bra was the same as "fornication." Then I think of what our imam says: "Show me what a man attacks, and I'll show you his sin."

Eleven

We get home midafternoon. Mom practically has a hemorrhage. She was taking a nap, heard me downstairs, and thought I was a burglar. "What happened to your weekend?"

"Andy's folks had to go away," I shrug. "If we'd stayed, we'd have been on our own. I said you and Dad wouldn't want that. Long story short, we came home." I hold my breath. It's not like it's a total lie. But it's not the total truth either.

"I'm so proud of you." Mom smiles. "You had the courage to make an unpopular choice. And you have loyal friends." She strokes my cheek like I'm a little kid. "It seems you boys have done some growing up. Your Dad and I won't have to worry so much."

Great. Can I feel more like a lying scum bag?

I go downstairs, unpack, and slip behind my computer. Andy and Marty are already online. Marty told his folks we're back early cuz the J's septic tank backed up. Nice. Andy's sorry about his meltdown and wishes he'd hung in. Now he's stuck alone and he can't stop thinking about guess what. "Wanna keep me company? Come over for a swim? The heater's working; water's warm. We could see a movie after?"

I put my bathing suit on under my pants and grab a towel. A swim, that's all I want. But the snake in my ear keeps hissing about Dad maybe having an affair: *His cell phone records. Why not see if there's any calls to strange women in Toronto?*

Don't be stupid. There aren't any.

Why not be sure?

I go back to my computer. Dad's e-bills are in his e-mail account. Getting in is a snap. A while back, he showed Mom and me photos that Mr. Ibrahim, one of his friends from mosque, sent of his trip to Mecca. I watched him type his user ID: Arman158—his first name plus our house number. And his password: NARHET—*Tehran*, the city where he was born, spelled backward.

Dad's inbox has thousands of messages. I keep mine messy too, so if Dad snoops it'll be hard for him to find the gross-out links the guys send me.

The snake slithers inside me. *Is your dad the same? Trying to keep things and hide them at the same time?*

No. Just because I'm sneaky doesn't mean Dad is.

I want to stop now, to sign out, but my fingers type *AT&T* in the search window. Up come Dad's cell phone bills. I scan for Toronto. Allah forgive me. Spying on my father. It's evil.

It's not. You're doing it to protect your mom.

How? By acting like Dad's cheating?

If he's innocent, what's the problem?

The problem is I dishonor him!

Who's going to know?

Me. I'll know.

You deserve to know.

But I still won't know. If the woman's not from Toronto—like, if she's just flying in for the security conference too—she could be from anywhere. In that case, his calls wouldn't be to Toronto. Every long-distance number on his bill could be suspicious. Or if they're using e-mail, their hookup plans could be in any of the thousands of messages in his inbox.

True. And what if your dad has an e-mail account you don't know about? Or what if they use text messaging?

AAAH! I want to rip the snake out of my head. But before I can, it strikes.

Three Toronto numbers leap off the screen. Does one of them belong to her? I write them down, kick myself. Why did I have to spy? I could've pretended everything was fine. Not now. *Now* I have to check these numbers out, or go insane.

I can't call from here: Dad pays my cell bill, he'd know what I did. I can't borrow Andy's or Marty's cells, either: I don't want them to know what I'm thinking.

Wait, I got it. Tonight, when the guys and I go to a movie, I'll sneak out during the trailers and call from a pay phone in the lobby.

I put my computer to sleep, grab my towel, and run upstairs. "I'm going to Andy's for a swim," I shout to Mom, back in the family room.

"That's nice," she hollers back. She blows her nose loudly. It figures; she's watching *Children of Heaven* again.

I throw open the front door. Brainwave. There'll be a file about the Toronto conference on Dad's computer. It'll have addresses and phone numbers for Toronto hotels and contacts. If my mystery numbers are there, it'll mean they're legit and I can relax. Sort of.

I slam the front door so Mom will think I've gone, and sneak up to Dad's office. If Mom catches me at his computer, what'll I tell her? Oh my god, stop now. Turn around, go to Andy's. I try, but the snake is a puppet master. Next thing I know, I'm inside Dad's office, the door shut behind me. I tiptoe to his desk. There's carpets on the floor, but every step's an earthquake. My heart beats so loud, I swear I'll go deaf.

I memorize how Dad's chair is placed, so I can put it back just right. I sit. To the left of his computer there's a small photo of him and me. It's under glass in a metal frame. I'm maybe six, seated on his lap. My head is tilted against his cheek. I'm tickling myself with his beard. We're laughing. That picture might as well be from another world.

I touch Dad's keypad. The screen lights up.

I click Documents, and open the folder marked Fall/Winter Conferences. Inside there's three PDFs: Toronto, September 19–22. Dallas, December 10–14. Washington, February 2–6.

I open the Toronto PDF, check the table of contents, scroll to the Hotels page. Near the top: "Hyatt Regency,

370 King Street West. Phone: 416-343-1234." Great. One of the three numbers. I'll bet he called to make sure his room was No Smoking.

I go to the Organizers page and spot the second number. It belongs to the Chair of the Events Committee.

There's only one number unaccounted for. Maybe it belongs to a workshop leader? I get their names from the Agenda pages and look them up on the Contact list. Nope.

No big deal. Maybe Dad planned a private get-together with a colleague? I check his e-calendar. Sure enough, he's logged a few meetings with male professors and research types. Each lists a cell. None matches my third number.

So what? I think. It means nothing. And that's when I notice something funny about the Sunday agenda. I double-check Dad's e-calendar against the official program. Same problem in both places: At 6:00 P.M. Sunday, there's cocktails and dinner at The Restaurant at the CN Tower. The special guest speaker is Dr. Augustus Brandt.

Augustus Brandt. Auggie. The speaker Dad supposedly had to replace on *Saturday*—tonight—the night we were supposed to be seeing the Jays. But Brandt's speech isn't tonight. It's on Sunday. *Tomorrow!*

I look at Dad's itinerary for tonight: "Blue Jays" on his calendar; "Evening Free" on the official program. I can't breathe.

Dad totally lied.

Why?

Twelve

After the swim, Andy and Marty come over for supper. Mom likes my friends, but she has a special soft spot for Marty. She was a chubby kid too, and knows all about the teasing.

What with Andy being a motormouth, Mom doesn't even think to ask for our Events of the Day. In no time, she's laughing so hard at his stories, she's practically gasping. Me, I don't hear any of it. It's like my mind is underwater. I struggle to break the surface, but that third phone number drags me down like a bag of cement.

It's nothing, I tell myself, nothing. When Dad fled from Iran, his grandma found a way to smuggle him to Canada. He was a teenager in Montreal, where he met Mom. They only emigrated here when he got his scholarship to NYU. So, hey, maybe Dad called an old friend who's in Toronto now. Maybe they could only get together Saturday night.

The snake stirs. *A friend is more important than a man's son?*

No, but Dad doesn't get to see his Canadian friends much. Me, he can take on a trip anytime.

So why didn't he say that? Besides, why wouldn't he want his friends to meet his son?

Maybe he would. But friends talk about the past. He might've thought I'd be bored.

He could have asked you. He didn't. Why? And why wouldn't he let your mom come either? She'd know his friends from the old days too. And by the way, why is the Jays game still in his calendar?

Who knows? Maybe he asked his friend to come to the game with us, then found he couldn't get an extra ticket. He had to save face.

By shafting you? Come on, Sami. Either your dad's having an affair, or he doesn't love you.

He does.

When was the last time he said it?

He doesn't have to say it.

Then when was the last time you felt it? This father–son

trip was your Mom's idea—not his—and you know it.
You embarrass him. You break his rules. You laugh at
him. Spy on him. What kind of son are you? No wonder
he hates you.

After supper, we leave for the movie.

The multiplex is packed. Our show has three crappy seats together up front, but there's two decent seats by the aisle. I tell Andy and Marty to take them. "Stiltz needs the legroom," I wink at Marty, and sit a few rows back.

No sooner am I by myself than I get major second thoughts about calling the third number. Who knows what I'm getting into? I should forget it, forget it, forget it. But the more I try to forget it, the more it's an itch I can't scratch.

The phones are near the concession stand. I tell the guys I'm going for popcorn, and take their orders so they'll stay in their seats. I don't want them to see me calling. They'd wonder what I was doing, why I wasn't using my cell.

As I leave the theater, I raise my hoodie. How weird is that? I mean, who's going to know or care that I'm making a phone call? But it's like I've got this neon sign flashing over my head: TRAITOR SON!

The phones are spaced around a column near the washrooms. I make a wide arc and pick one on the far side, away from the surveillance cameras over the concession's cash registers. Is this what happens to spies—they go paranoid?

I know this number by heart, but I take it out of my pocket and stare at it anyway.

I dial. The phone asks for money. Good thing I thought ahead and packed my coin jar in my knapsack. I drop in a ridiculous amount of quarters.

The phone rings. My temples burn. My hands shake. Any second, I may be hearing the voice of my Dad's girlfriend. What'll I say if she answers?

I panic. Hang up. The change fills the return cup. I scoop it out. A couple of coins fall to the floor. I pick them up and calm myself.

If the woman answers, I'll ask to speak to Dr. Sabiri. If there's a problem, like a jealous husband, I'll say, "Sorry, wrong number." If she calls Dad to the phone, I'll hang up.

I redial. Drop the change. Hear a ring. Someone lifts the receiver. I hang up.

What kind of baby am I?

I better wait a few minutes before calling again. If anyone answers now, they'll be pissed at the false rings.

I arc back into the corner shadows and join the crowd at the popcorn lines.

I bring Andy and Marty their drinks and munchies as the trailers start.

"I'm going to the can," I whisper—as if they care—and run back to the lobby. There's a man at the phones. He doesn't leave. I'll try later.

I slip out twice more, but there's always somebody hanging around. When our movie ends, the halls and lobby are too packed to do anything but flood out with the flow.

Next morning, Sunday, Mom drives us to Rochester for a charity thing at the mosque. While Mom's having refreshments in the basement with the rest of the congregation, I slip upstairs to the greeting area. It's empty. I go to the phones to the right of the men's entrance. I dial. Drop in the change. Grip the phone panel so I won't chicken out.

After two rings, a woman's voice, perky, twenty-something: "There's nobody here. You know what to do." Beep.

I hang up. Go to the washroom. Douse my face in ice-cold water.

The voice in my head won't stop. *You know what to do.* It gets louder and louder, a loop in my brain: *You know what to do. You know what to do.*

The thing is, I don't.

Thirteen

I bike to school Monday morning. Friday seems like years ago, but not to Eddy Duh Turd. He and five of his football buddies are waiting outside the Academy gates; two in his BMW, the others in his pal Mark Greeley's SUV. I pretend not to notice and swing past them onto Roosevelt Trail.

They follow me, Eddy in the lead. Eddy doesn't rev his engine, honk his horn, or say a word. Just purrs along a few feet behind my rear tire. I speed up, he speeds up; I slow down, he slows down. Halfway along the track, he pulls up beside me. "Yo, sand monkey, wuzzup?" he calls out the window. "I said I'd be waiting for you. Why did you disappear?"

I pedal faster.

"You too chicken to talk?"

His buddies makes cluck sounds. Eddy squeezes me toward the curb. Let him try and push me off the road; my bike'll scrape the shit out of his paint job.

Eddy knows it too. He speeds ahead, brakes. I'm caught between his BMW and the SUV. The gang spills out of the cars. I try to dodge them. They box me in.

I stop. "What do you want?"

"Guess." Eddy shoves me hard. I fall over, tangled up in my bike. He stomps on the spokes of my front tire. I scramble free, but he kicks me onto my back, jumps on top, and pins my hands to the ground. His crew circles us.

"Little reminder, sand monkey," he says. "When you finally see McGregor, I never said a word to you in History. You swore at me for nothing. Got it? And by the way," he knees me in the gut, "next time I tell you to meet me and my boys, you be there."

"Harrison!" It's Mr. Bernstein. His Corolla's pulled up beside us.

Eddy leaps off me. His crew backs away. I get up.

"What's going on?" Mr. Bernstein says.

I brush off my pants. "No big deal, sir. I crashed my

bike. They were helping me."

Mr. Bernstein isn't buying. "Six on one, Harrison." He shakes his head in disgust.

"I thought you liked seeing guys on top of each other," Eddy mutters.

Snickers from the gang.

Mr. Bernstein pretends not to hear. "An assault on school property. You boys can expect a very serious chat with the vice principal."

"Oh yeah? Sabiri says everything's fine. And we'll all back each other up." Eddy smirks. "Besides, my dad's on the Academy board. See the new scoreboard on the football field? We all know who paid for it. So you see, sir, I'd be careful what I said if I were you. My dad knows all about you. Make up a story, and we will too."

"Don't pull that crap with me," Mr. Bernstein snaps. "Now move it."

Eddy's gang returns to their cars.

"Watch your back," Eddy whispers. I don't know if the message is for me or Mr. Bernstein. Eddy slouches into his front seat. The engines rev, and he and his gang take off.

Mr. Bernstein puts a hand on my shoulder. "You sure you're all right?"

I nod.

"It's tough, isn't it?" he says gently.

"What?"

"The names. The everything." He gives a wry smile. "I was raised in Utah."

For a second, we're on the same planet. I grin.

"Want a ride up the hill? Your bike's pretty banged up. We can put it in my trunk."

"I'm okay, thanks." I'm scared of Eddy coming back for me. But I'm even more scared of anyone thinking I need protection—not to mention seeing me get out of Mr. Bernstein's car. I flush with shame. I like Mr. Bernstein. Why do I care what these guys think? They're idiots.

Mr. Bernstein pauses. "I'd like you to tell Mr. McGregor what happened."

"Nothing happened, sir."

"That's not true. We both know it."

I toe the ground. "Sir, I know you're trying to help, but here's the thing. There's a zero-tolerance policy for fighting. If I tell, I'd get suspended too. My dad would kill me."

Mr. Bernstein puts up a hand. "Zero tolerance doesn't apply to bullying."

"Who says it was bullying? You didn't see it, sir. You guessed. Which makes it my word against six Academy athletes. Can you imagine Mr. McGregor suspending a quarter of the football team midseason? Especially when their parents are like Eddy's?"

Mr. Bernstein looks deep in my eyes. "Sami, if you don't speak up, the office won't act and I can't help you. But if you *do*, at the very least, Harrison and the others will have a note in their files."

"A lot of good that'll do me, biking home. Or at the mall. Or anytime I'm alone. They'll get me big-time. Where will you be then, sir?"

His eyes cloud. "Life can be tough, Sami. But hiding only makes things worse. In the end, no matter how hard you try, you can't hide from yourself. Trust me." He gets into his car. "See you in class." And he's gone.

I push my bike up the hill and lock it at the side of the school. I think about going to the can to clean the scrape on my hand, check my ribs for bruises, clear my head. But Eddy or one of his gang could trap me and finish what they started.

I catch Mitchell squatting by our lockers, studying. His lips are moving overtime.

"Hey, Mitchell."

Mitchell brushes the hair off his face. "Whoa. What happened to you?"

"Eddy. Watch the can door for me, will you? If you see Eddy coming, holler."

Mitchell squirms. "There's a math test."

"So what? Are you my friend or not?"

"Okay, okay."

He hangs a million miles away, by the drinking fountain, while I go in to clean up. When I come out, he's gone.

I'm called to the office right after the anthem. Vice Principal McGregor makes me wait on the bench by the sign-in counter for two hours. It's not like he's busy. Every twenty minutes or so, he strolls out of his inner sanctum to shoot the breeze with his secretary. I guess having me wait makes him feel important. Eddy saunters by between periods one and two. He gives me the cut-eye through the hall window. I'm like a guppy in a shark tank. At last, in the middle of period two, the secretary says, "The vice principal will see you now." Right. Like he hasn't seen me all morning.

I step into his office. Mr. McGregor's in his shirtsleeves, propped back in his chair, hands clasped behind his head. It's quite a sight. McGregor's got bigger man-boobs than Marty. He nods at the chair opposite his desk. I sit. He looks through me, like he's watching TV with the sound off. I wrap my feet under my chair, shift around a bit, and try not to stare at the tufts of red belly hair curling out from between the shirt buttons over his gut.

"We had an appointment Friday afternoon," Mr. McGregor says at last.

"I forgot."

"You forgot." Mr. McGregor lets the words sink in. "You were summoned from class. And you forgot? Ten minutes later, I personally called you from the front steps. Again, you forgot?"

"Sir, I'm sorry, sir, I had a lot on my mind, really, I didn't hear you, sorry."

Pause. "Respect," Mr. McGregor says. "Respect is the cornerstone of life at this Academy." He picks up a pen. "It's the cornerstone of life." He taps the pen three times on his doodle pad, like he's profound or something.

"Yes, sir."

"Eddy Harrison tells me you swore at him. Did you?"

"I don't know. Maybe."

"Maybe you did or maybe you didn't?"

"I . . . I guess maybe I did."

"Why?"

"No reason."

"There must be a reason."

"I don't remember."

Mr. McGregor rolls back in his chair. There's a rim of sweat under his man-boobs. "Can you at least remember this morning?"

"It depends. What about this morning?"

A scary pause. "The Academy has a zero-tolerance policy for violence. You're aware of it?"

I flash on me getting expelled, Dad going bananas. "Yes," I whisper.

"So perhaps you'd like to tell me what happened on Roosevelt Trail?"

"N-nothing, sir."

"Nothing?"

"No, sir. Nothing."

"You weren't in a fight with Harrison?"

"No, sir. Not really, sir. I don't care what Mr. Bernstein told you."

"Who says he told me anything?" Mr. McGregor bunches his bushy eyebrows. "What would he have told me?"

"I don't know. I'm not sure." I wriggle like a fish on a hook.

McGregor reels me in, nice and slow. "Harrison reports

that you were zigzagging your bike in the middle of the road. He asked you to move to the side, so he and his friends could drive by. You turned your head, insulted his family, and crashed into the curb. When he came to help you up, you blamed him for the accident and accused him of attacking you. Which is why he stepped forward, to clear his name in advance. Is Harrison's account accurate?"

"I . . . I forget."

"Forgetting is a habit with you, isn't it, Sabiri? A theme."

I stare at the carpet.

"Look at me when I talk to you."

I glance back up.

"When Harrison was called to my office Friday, he came right away," Mr. McGregor says. "You, on the other hand, chose to run. Today you answer every question with 'I don't know' or 'I can't remember.' Your cowardice speaks to your character, Sabiri."

"Yes, sir," I mumble.

Mr. McGregor sticks his head into the outer office and asks his secretary to send for Eddy. While we wait for Duh Turd, he paces the office, lecturing me on how I have to obey the rules, submit to authority, answer questions, and not waste his time.

Eddy shows up as the lunch bell rings.

McGregor makes us shake hands, then gives us a cold once-over. "No action will be taken regarding this morning's incident. But I've made note of it for future reference. In the meantime, Sabiri, for running away, swearing, and evasiveness, you will serve one-hour detentions for the rest of this week, in the main office before class. Harrison, for the remark overheard by Mr. Bernstein, you get a one-hour detention to be served now."

Eddy and I leave the vice principal's office. He flops on the bench to do his time.

"I'll get you for this," he says under his breath.

"For what? I didn't do anything."

"Tell it to the undertaker."

After lunch, I get to period three before Eddy's detention ends. At the last period change, though, I see Eddy coming toward me. Thank God I'm short and skinny. I slip sideways through the mobs in the corridors, zipping from one tall person to the next. It's like I'm in a video game: *Academy Hell Race.*

I make it to History and catch a break. Mr. Bernstein's changed the seating plan. He's moved Eddy to the back corner: Siberia. Me, he's moved to the front by the door, where I'll have a chance to escape at the end of class. Luckily, he's shifted other guys too, so it's not obvious he made the change for me.

End of the day, another break. Eddy's got football practice. I wait till Mitchell tells me he's doing warm-ups, then walk my bike home as fast as I can. As I pass the field, I hear Eddy's crew chant: "Sa-*bi*-ri. Sa-*bi*-ri. Sa-*bi*-ri."

At least I'll be safe at home, I think.

But I'm not.

Fourteen

Dad's already arrived home when I wheel in. His morning tour of Toronto's new high-security bio lab got canceled, and he managed to catch an early flight. There's wrapped gifts in the living room. Guilt much?

"Great conference, great city," Dad says. "I'll take you soon." Sure. And introduce me to your secret girlfriend while you're at it.

"How did the speech go?" I ask innocently.

Dad doesn't miss a beat. "Terrific, thanks. Auggie phoned last night to say he'd heard great things on the grapevine."

"So Dr. Brandt's out of the hospital?"

Dad gives me a funny look. "Never in. Gallstones, I think. May we be spared, Inshallah." He's smooth, my dad. "Come, open your presents."

Mom gets a bunch of body lotions and bath oils. Apricot, lavender, and eucalyptus. She has us smell them. They come from France. Three cheers for the duty-free shop.

I open my box. There's a navy cotton hoodie with TORONTO stitched across the front in big felt letters. "Gee, thanks." I put it aside.

"Aren't you going to try it on?"

"Why? It's not like I went."

"Sami," Mom says with this sharp Your-Dad-Just-Got-Home-And-He's-Trying-So-Don't-Start-In-Okay look.

"Sorry." I sigh. "It's really nice. I'm tired is all." And I put it on and try to smile while Dad takes pictures of the three of us in every possible combination times a million. He only lets up when Mom mentions the lamb stew will be ready soon, so maybe we should tidy up and do prayers.

I recite Maghrib, but the whole time I'm thinking, How did Dad learn to be such a good liar? When else has he lied? And what was he doing on Saturday night? I wonder through supper too, as I stuff my face with lamb korma and bluff my way through half-fake Events Of The

Weekend, like how I played video games Friday night, went to a movie at the mall on Saturday, and studied all Sunday.

The doorbell rings.

Dad answers. Mom and I keep eating. I figure it's Jehovah's Witnesses. Mom bets it's the real estate salesman from up the street. We're both wrong.

"Can I help you?" Dad's voice is dry and high-pitched, like he's trying a little too hard to sound normal.

We hear a couple of men's voices, low and serious.

"Come in, come in," Dad says. "Neda? Sami? We have visitors."

I run to the front hall and practically crap my pants. These men aren't visitors. They're cops. Two locals. Their squad car is sitting in the driveway.

"Don't worry about your shoes," Mom says, like the cops really care about her floors. "Sorry, the place is such a mess."

Dad leads us all into the family room. He and Mom bunch together on the sectional and smile like they're entertaining friends from the golf club. I sit off to the side. To keep from getting scared, I pretend I'm watching a TV show. A bad TV show. I mean, shouldn't one of them stay at the front door in case there's more of us upstairs, planning a sneak attack?

Anyway, the younger cop's kind of lanky, with a big Adam's apple. He stands with his right hand lazing on his gun belt, checking our rolled prayer rugs when he thinks no one's watching. The older cop has a burn scar on his left cheek, where it looks like he got smashed by a hot iron or something. He sits on the ottoman, at a right angle to his partner, and pulls out a notepad.

"So what can we do for you?" Dad asks.

"Would you like some coffee?" Mom offers.

"No, thanks," Scarface says. "New York State Police asked us to drop by." He sees Dad take Mom's hand. "Relax, relax. There's nothing to worry about. Yet."

"Yet?"

"Over the weekend, your son was caught trespassing on private property in the Thousand Islands."

"You've made a mistake," Dad says. "He was here with my wife." Dad looks to Mom to back him up. Mom looks to me for an explanation. My mouth bobs open and shut.

"You're 'Mohammed Sami Sabiri'?" Scarface asks me, looking up from his notes. "You're acquainted with Martin Pratt and Andrew Johnson?"

I nod. About this TV show—I want to change channels.

Scarface turns to my folks. "These names, along with addresses, were taken by the Stillman family's caretaker. The family doesn't wish to press charges, but they want the partying on their land to stop before it gets out of hand. Over the past month, the caretaker's found beer cans, condoms, drug paraphernalia. We're not saying your son's involved with any of that"—he looks back to me—"but keep your nose clean. Okay?"

"Some friendly advice," Lanky nods to Dad, "covering up for your kid is never a good idea."

"I don't. I—"

"Yeah, yeah, I know," Lanky says. "Enough said."

The cops shake our hands. Mom shows them out. Dad sinks into the sectional like his guts have been ripped out. I try to say something, but he holds up his hand without looking at me.

"Thanks for your time," from Scarface as he leaves. "You take care, now."

"Thanks, yes, you as well," Mom says. "And don't worry, we'll keep an eye on Sami."

The front door closes. Mom returns. She clears her throat. "After you canceled Sami's trip to Toronto, he was invited to the Johnsons' cottage. I gave permission."

Dad stares so hard at the potpourri bowl on the coffee

table, I expect it to explode. "Why didn't you tell me?"

"I should have. I'm sorry."

"And what about tonight?" His eyes are wounded. "To my face, he said he stayed home and played video games Friday. Why did he lie? Why did you let him?" Dad clutches his head in his hands. "My God! The police at our door!"

"Dad—"

"Enough! Alcohol. Condoms. Drugs. What have you been up to? How long has it been going on?"

"Dad, nothing's been going on."

"Police don't come to a home for nothing."

"Look, we went to an island. We thought it was okay. Andy and Marty, they had a couple of beers, that's all. I had a soda. The other stuff wasn't us."

"Why should I believe you?"

"Because it's the truth."

"Hah!" Dad claps his hands. "You're grounded. I will personally drive you to school for your nine o'clock classes. And I will personally pick you up after I finish work. You will wait for me, studying, in the Academy library. Understood?"

"Yes . . . ," I whisper. "But for this week . . . this week . . ."

"Speak up. What about this week?"

I shrink into myself. "This week, can I be at school at eight?"

"No," Dad shakes his head fiercely. "There'll be no horsing around in the halls. You're in enough trouble already."

"That's just it," I say. "I have to be there. I have detentions. From the vice principal."

"What?" Dad whirls on Mom. "Did you know about this too?"

"No, Dad," I jump in. "I didn't say a word. And anyway, it's not my fault. Stuff happened, but not like the vice principal thinks. Eddy Harrison, he told lies about me."

"Lies!" Dad yells. "Lies, lies, lies! It's all lies with you! Secrets and lies!"

"Look who's talking!" I hear the words. Are they still in my head? Or did I actually say them?

Dad backs up, breathing heavy. I guess I said them.

"What do you mean?" he dares me.

If I say what I know . . . what I think . . .

I glance over at Mom. She's afraid. What does she know, think?

"I said, what do you mean?" Dad repeats.

I look straight at him. "Guess."

There's a flicker of fear in his eyes.

Then—

I see Dad throw back his shoulders.

I hear him say, "I have no son."

I see him storm from the room.

And I see Mom look at me, bewildered.

I look back, ashamed. Ashamed for having lied to her, for bringing on the cops, for opening a door into a place we're all afraid to go.

Then I run. Run downstairs to my room. Dive under my covers. Bury my head under my pillow in the pitch dark of the basement night.

But no matter how hard I press it to my ears, or squeeze my eyes tight shut, nothing can make the world go away.

Fifteen

Andy and Marty text me around midnight. They're so lucky. The cops came by their places too. But they're not grounded. Andy's mom was fried on Xanax and vodka chasers. She kept telling Lanky how good he looked in his uniform, and actually asked Scarface what happened to his face. Battery acid at a chop shop raid, apparently.

Over at Marty's, Mister Bubbles went for Lanky's ankles. When they left, Marty's mom went bananas, till his dad reminded her how they were arrested for skinny-dipping in a public pool after their high school graduation, and burst into a rousing rendition of "Thanks for the Memories!" Me, I can't picture my folks skinny-dipping, ever. Naked parents? I'd rather go blind.

Anyway, life's cool at casa Johnson and casa Pratt. But at casa Sabiri, forget it.

Dad doesn't say a word to me at morning prayers, breakfast, or on the drive to the Academy.

We arrive in the office at ten to eight. Mr. McGregor fills Dad in about me running away when I was called to his office. He says the incident on Roosevelt Trail is being investigated, and he'll try to keep it out of my official record.

Dad apologizes for my behavior. "He wasn't raised this way. Please let us know if he's involved in any other mischief. My wife and I will support whatever punishment you see fit."

I want to scream how it's all garbage, but what's the point? Eddy can shovel bullshit till the cows come home, and his father eats it up. My dad? No way. He won't even believe the truth.

"My wife and I appreciate your efforts with our son," he says, all stiff and grave like he's holding it together at a funeral. "It's always a shock when one's child . . ." He pauses, collects himself. "We'll do our best to see that he's never a problem for you again." He tries to look at me, but he can't. He walks out of the office like I'm dead.

* * *

I survive morning classes. But when I step into the cafeteria, I smell trouble. Eddy and his gang are hunched over their table, staring at me. For once, I'm glad Mom makes me a halal lunch; I don't have to be a target in the serving line.

I head to my place in the far corner with the Loser Lunch Bunch. They eat fast and head to the library before the paper bags start flying. But today they're AWOL, except for Mitchell. He buries his head in his book and pretends he hasn't seen me.

When I reach my chair, I know why. Two words are carved in the table where I sit:

SABIRI SUX

The gashes are scribbled in with magic marker. There's no way to get them out. They'll be there forever.

I want to throw up. I mean, I always knew I was hated. But this makes it real. Real for everyone to see. I have to leave. Now. I can't let them see me cry.

I turn to go. Eddy's gang gets up. They're grinning. I sit down. They sit down too. I spend the rest of the period trying not to think about the carving under my lunch bag, or Eddy's gang staring at me from across the room.

The bell rings. I dash through the cafeteria doors to Science before Eddy can catch me.

I don't hear anything Mr. Carson says. Just stare at the yogurt that dribbled into his beard at lunch, and worry about how I'll get to History without being nabbed by Eddy.

Somehow I make it.

Mr. Bernstein's moved on from ancient witch trials to "the witch hunts of the Cold War: a time of terror that destroyed the innocent along with the guilty." He talks about the nightmare of being falsely accused. The horror of knowing you could be damned by circumstantial evidence and classified secrets based on fears, rumors, and lies.

It makes me think of everything that looks true but isn't. Like Andy's happy family. And mine. And about things that are partly true, except that the untrue parts turn the true parts inside out. Like what my folks think happened on Hermit Island. And I think about Dad. Things that I know, and things that I don't know, except in my heart.

All of a sudden, I don't feel so good. I raise my hand. "Can I go to the washroom?"

Mr. Bernstein nods. As I head out the door, Eddy asks to go too.

"I don't think so," Bernstein says drily.

I head down the second-floor hallway to the stairwell at the rear east end of the school. My secret spot is the cubbyhole under the stairs on the first floor. I showed it to Dad at last year's open house, told him it's where I do my noon prayers. It's a great hideout. Way better than the can. For one thing, it doesn't stink. For another, it's totally safe: Even when classes are changing, no one can see you. Best of all, it's never checked by custodians or teachers. I know because last spring, as an experiment, I left a Mars bar wrapper crumpled up in the corner. It was still there in June.

I push open the glass stairwell doors and listen for the sound of footsteps coming up. Silence. Great. I scoot down and slide into my spot. My back slouches into the brick wall; my feet slide forward along the granite floor till my toes touch the underside of the stairs.

I pull my cell out of my pants pocket and text Andy. No reply. When Andy's in class, he leaves his cell on pulse. I figure he must be taking a test or something.

That's okay. I melt into the peace and quiet. There's no one to spy on me. No one to jab me in the back, throw spit balls at me, or call me names. I'm invisible. I close my eyes. My shoulders drop. I breathe—slow, slower—and float off into the private world behind my eyelids.

I'm in the past. At my madrassa. Dad's smiling at me as I kneel in front of my old teacher, Mr. Neriwal, and recite my first verses of the Qur'an.

And now I see Dad carrying me home. I'm even younger, half asleep in his arms. He nuzzles my cheek with his nose.

And now it's winter. We're on the ice rink Dad made for me in the backyard when I was two. I'm in tiny little skates, bundled up in my snowsuit, scarf, and leggings, and I'm holding onto the seat of a kitchen chair. Dad pulls the chair gently, gently across the ice. I slide along, laughing, as Mom records us on video.

Am I remembering what happened, or just remembering the movies I saw later? I don't care. I want to stay here forever. I'm back in the days when Dad loved me and we were happy.

The final bell wakes me up.

I hear movement in the halls beyond the stairwell. I roll out of my cubbyhole, and run up to the second floor—first, so no one will see my hiding place; second, to reach Mr. Bernstein's room before he locks up with all my stuff inside.

I pass Mitchell. "Eddy's looking for you," he says.

"Where?"

"Don't know."

Gotta move fast. I rush into Mr. Bernstein's room. He's at his filing cabinet. I don't look at him, just go for my books. I'm hoping he'll let me escape, but he doesn't.

"Sami," he says without looking up, "next time you need to clear your head, tell me you're sick, and I'll write you a note. If you just take off, I look bad."

"Sorry."

"And Sami . . ." He closes the cabinet and turns around, a sheaf of worksheets in his hand. "Sami, if you ever need to talk, I'm here. You know that, right?"

"I do," I nod. "Yes. Thanks." I back out of the room, shuffling and bowing.

Eddy's waiting for me, a classroom away, slouched against the lockers on the opposite side of the hall. He puts two fingers to his eyes and points at me.

"What?" I toss my chin and head to the library. I make sure not to walk too fast; don't want him thinking I'm scared. Still, I go fast enough that he'll have to run to catch me. He won't do that, will he? There's too many teachers around, aren't there?

I want to look around to see if Eddy's catching up, but I don't. To stay safe, you gotta stay cool.

I keep my eyes focused straight ahead till I reach the library. Inside, I take a study nook by the wall near the book checkout, and start doing my homework.

Eddy watches me through the glass doors. He's grinning. "You're trapped," he mouths on the other side of the glass.

I laugh and blow him a kiss. That pisses him off good.

I can't wait to see his face when Dad comes to pick me up. A parental limo service: the one good thing about being grounded.

Eddy keeps his distance Wednesday and Thursday. But I see his BMW outside the Academy gates each morning when Dad drops me off and in the afternoon when he picks me up. Dad doesn't notice. He's too busy being silent.

Friday morning I find an envelope wedged through the crack of my locker. Inside is a one-sheet, computer printout:

THINK DADDY CAN SAVE YOUR ASS?
WE KNOW WHERE YOU LIVE.

Sixteen

The whole weekend, I'm stuck inside. Dad says I can't have anyone over, meaning Andy and Marty, who are apparently the spawn of Satan. As in, "Those Boys Have Been Trouble From Day One." It's worse than prison: Even murderers get visitors. At least I can talk to the guys by cell. I tell them about Eddy's note.

"He's just messing with your head," Andy says. "No way he'd come on your property."

All the same, I make sure the curtains in the family room are closed after dark. I'm creeped he might spy on me from the golf course.

Monday, it's back to Academy Hell Race. By now I know I'm fine as long as I stay in the open with people around.

At lunch, I head to my corner in the caf. I've decided to fix Eddy's woodworking: SABIRI SUX.

Mitchell's moved his studying to the far end of the table. "I can sit with you," he says, "but I don't want anyone to think we're talking."

"Then you should stop moving your lips when you read."

Mitchell gets this panicked look and covers his mouth with both hands.

I get to work. First, I line my books around the SABIRI SUX carving so no one'll see what I'm doing—especially Mr. Carson, who's on caf duty. Then I pull Dad's chisel out of my knapsack. I start to connect the ends of the Ss, so they look like 8s.

Mitchell glances over. "What are you doing?"

"What does it look like?"

He goes clammy. "Stop it. You'll get us in trouble."

"How?"

"Defacing school property."

"Gimme a break. It's already defaced." I turn each I into a T.

Mitchell twitches so bad you'd swear he was on crack. "I'm serious, Sammy. I don't want to get suspended."

"You won't. You're just studying."

"Yeah, but I know what you're doing. I'll be an accessory after the fact."

I roll my eyes. "Mitchell, grow up. Sit somewhere else."

"But everyone knows I sit here."

I decide to ignore him. The *U* in SUX looks like a *V*. I put a line on top and turn it into a triangle. Mitchell vanishes. Good.

I put a line under the *A*, making it a little triangle in a big triangle, and lines at the top and bottom of the *X*, turning it into a kind of hourglass. Then I take out a marker and scribble in the gouges.

"What do you think you're doing, Sabiri?" It's Mr. Carson, his beard flecked with egg salad. I see Mitchell, five tables over, trying to hide. The snitch. Like, I know he was the one who ratted me out. Don't I?

I'm brought to the vice principal's office. I try to explain. Mr. McGregor visits the scene of the crime. He says the carving doesn't look like SABIRI SUX; it looks like "premeditated vandalism."

"I know it doesn't look like SABIRI SUX. I changed it. That was the point."

"Why didn't you report it?"

"I was embarrassed."

"Why didn't anyone else report it?"

"Why would they? It's not like it was their name written there." Plus, I think, what supervising teacher wants to look slack? And why would a custodian bother? It'd just be more crap to deal with.

I try to get Mitchell to be my witness about how I was just trying to fix my name being gouged, but he's too scared. He says he never saw anything, except what he told Mr. Carson: "Please, sir. I'm not an accessory, sir." Hey, Mitchell, you're right. You're not an accessory. You're an asshole.

Mr. McGregor slaps me with a rest-of-the-week suspension for bringing a weapon to school—Dad's chisel—and defacing Academy property. I also get an official report in my school file, a letter to my parents with a bill for the damage, and a warning that the next incident will result in expulsion.

Dad hits the roof. He's already had daily migraines since coming back from Toronto, thanks to my earlier run-ins with the law and Mr. McGregor. Like, it couldn't possibly have anything to do with his secret girlfriend, right? But with my suspension, he goes from Tylenol to Demerol.

He also announces, "Starting today your mother and

I will be doing random checks of your room. We'll be looking for alcohol, drugs, condoms, weapons, and any other mischief you might be up to." With that he takes a hammer and screwdriver, and pops the hinge pins on my bedroom door.

"Dad?" I say. "There's this little thing called privacy."

"Why do you need privacy? Do you have something to hide?"

"That's not the point. It's sort of in the Constitution, Dad. Along with, oh, I don't know, freedom?"

"Freedom requires responsibility," he glares. "You should have thought of that before you broke our trust."

I throw my arms in the air. "I went to a cottage unsupervised. I trespassed on an abandoned island. It was wrong. I'm sorry. But as for the serious stuff, I'm innocent."

"What crook says he's guilty?" Dad demands.

"Dad. Listen. There's explanations."

"No doubt." If his eyes were fists they'd pound me. He pulls the door loose and carries it behind the furnace.

I turn to Mom. "This isn't fair."

Mom holds up a hand. She walks upstairs.

Great. I'm in lockdown.

Seventeen

It's one A.M. Thursday night—well, early Friday morning, technically. Whatever. This time tomorrow, my suspension will be history. It's been a slice. Nonstop video games and web surfing. I should maybe get suspended more often.

Mind you, the surveillance sucks. Mom's taken the evening shift so she can watch me during the day. She gets home at eleven and goes straight to bed. Dad's already asleep. But I can't sneak out; they've changed the security code. If I try to leave without them knowing, the alarm'll go off.

One plus is Dad's Demerol. When his head hits the pillow, he's history. So as soon as Mom crashes, I get uncensored webcam visits with Andy and Marty. No texting, just talk. They don't worry about being heard either. Marty's dad snores so loud, his mom sleeps through anything. And Andy's alone upstairs: His dad's officially out of the house, and his mom's adrift in the rec room La-Z-Boy, tuned to the Home Shopping Network.

So anyway, it's one A.M. and the three of us are online. Andy and I are totally grossed out: Marty's mooning the screen. I don't know whether to laugh or gag. We're talking fifty pounds of marbled lard with a couple of cherry-sized zits.

Marty's hands move his cheeks so it looks like his butt is talking: "This is your father, Sammy. I think I gotta sneeze." The ass-puppet rips a fart.

"You pig!" I wave my hands like I can smell it over the ether.

Andy goes for a pee break. Marty and I horse around while he's gone. It's weird. Hermit Island sucked so bad that we bonded again. Now we're buddies again like in the old days.

Suddenly, Andy's back. "Sammy!" he gasps. "I looked out the bathroom window. There's strangers down on the golf course, other side of your hedge!"

"What?"

"At least five or six of them. It's dark, they're wearing black, I can't tell how many for sure."

"Very funny."

"No kidding, bro. They're facing your house. I think they've got dogs."

"If you're trying to scare me, Andy, quit it."

"I'm not. It's what I saw."

My guts melt. "You said Eddy'd never come on my property."

"Who says it's Eddy?"

"Who else would it be?"

"Want me to call the cops?" Marty asks.

"No," I say. "They're the last thing I need."

"What, then?"

"I'm gonna check it out."

"I got your back," Andy says. "I'll be in the can with my cell. Any trouble, it's 911, whether you like it or not."

"What about me? What do I do?" from Marty.

"Sit tight," Andy says.

I turn off my light, and feel my way to the basement stairs. I know my way to the kitchen by heart. Upstairs is completely dark, except for the spill from the street lamp, splashing across the hall floor from the bay window in the living room. I tiptoe to the family room, back pressed to the wall.

I have a flash of Andy and Marty laughing on their webcams. If this is a joke . . .

The curtains on the French doors leading out to the patio are closed.

I hear a sound. Can't make it out. I stand stock-still. It stops. I edge forward, barely daring to breathe. Eddy. His gang. They wouldn't. They couldn't. Then I flash on them spray-painting our back wall.

They could.

I run to the French doors. Throw open the curtains. Nothing. Nobody. The yard's empty.

I back up toward the kitchen, go to the window on my right. I peek between the curtains. From the corner of my eye, I see a red dot appear on the fabric. It disappears. Where did it go? Suddenly, the beam hits my eyes. What the hell? Holy shit, I'm caught in a scope!

I drop to the floor. "Mom! Dad! Help!"

I roll to the French doors to close those curtains too. Two masked men leap into view. They boot the panes by the locks. The doors smash open. They charge in.

Our alarm goes off.

I scramble down the hall. "MOM! DAD!"

I'm tackled, foot of the stairs. My arm yanks up behind me.

I see Mom at the top. She's caught in the beam of a flashlight.

Mom screams. Men and dogs run up after her. She races toward the bedroom. Two of the men grab her and drag her into the office.

"MOM!!!"

A knee drops on my neck.

"FBI! FREEZE!"

PART THREE

PART THREE

Eighteen

The world's a blur of shouts. Shadows. Boots. Dogs.

"FB—?"

"I SAID FREEZE!"

The knee jams into my face. It burns my left cheek into the carpet. Squashes into my eye.

Can't breathe. Can't see. Except—

Dad in a headlock. Men crowded around him. Attack dogs at the ready.

Dad's dazed from the Demerol. "Who—? What—?"

They hustle him down the stairs, out the front door. The dogs follow, straining their leads.

"Why???" Dad cries out. He disappears into the night.

In the distance, sirens. Cops. Andy. He must've made the call.

Now lights. Lights everywhere. I blink in the glare. See an army of agents tromping up and down the stairs. Dad's computer carted away. His scanner. Drawers. Files.

And I'm suddenly airborne. Up on my toes, my arms half out of their sockets. A hand grips my head from behind. Forces it down into my chest. I'm whirled around, forced to the kitchen, down the basement stairs into my room.

Marty's face is on my monitor. His eyes go wild when he sees me. Somebody yanks out the plug. The screen goes blank. Oh my god! They're taking my computer.

"Wait! Don't! It's got my homework!"

It's got my homework?

Two men with rubber gloves empty my desk. Others tear down my posters, rip open my mattress.

"What are you looking for? What?"

Fingers dig under my collarbone. I crumple.

My chair gets spun from behind. I face a bare wall.

Through the open door, I hear crashes upstairs in the kitchen and family room, and down the corridor in Dad's workshop. A whine of drills. A smash of axes, maybe crowbars. A tide of agents floods by with plastic bags from the downstairs freezer, plus Dad's toolbox and who knows what else.

Are the men who wrecked my room still here? Is anybody here? Am I alone? I want to turn around, to see, to know, but I'm afraid. I'm—

I smell the stink of stale cigar smoke. Hear my two folding chairs scrape across the floor. One stops behind me, to my left. The other bangs down to my right.

Silence.

Whoever's there, they're staring at the center of the back of my head. It's as if my skull is burning. Like their eyes are drilling their way into my brain.

"What's going on?"

A long pause. Then a man's voice from the chair to my left: "We know everything, Sami."

I hesitate. "How do you know my name?"

"You weren't listening, Sami. We know everything."

The man to my right shifts in his chair. His butt makes a sound on the plastic seat cover. "Is there something you'd like to tell us?" Wait, I was wrong. This voice, it isn't a man—it's a woman. "If you tell us, it'll make things easier," she says.

I think: If you know everything, what can I tell you?

"Can I turn around?"

"No."

I try to picture them. I can't. They're like voices in a nightmare, at the end of a dark alley; wherever you turn to run, it's always the alley, with them at the end of it.

"Why are you here?" I whisper.

"You know."

"I don't!"

The man snorts. I hear him get up, walk slowly around my room. Every so often he stops. Why? What's got his attention?

"Am I in trouble?"

"Not if you cooperate," the woman says.

"How? I don't even know what you want."

"The truth," the man says. He's over by my dresser.

"The truth about what?" The snake slithers in my guts. I try not to panic. "Is this about Toronto?" I want to bite off my tongue.

"Toronto?" the man says. "What do you know about Toronto?"

"Nothing."

"Then why did you say it?"

"It just came out."

"Funny thing to think of, Toronto." He sits. "Funny thing to say, out of the blue."

"It's not," I say. "It's— Me and my dad— We were going to see the Jays and the Leafs, and— Look, should I have a lawyer?"

"Why do you need a lawyer?" the woman asks.

"Because, I guess, I mean, I thought—"

"Tell us," she says calmly. "We don't want to make things hard for you."

The snake coils in my belly. *This IS about Toronto. It's about your dad. His lies. His secret phone number.*

I don't know that.

So tell them. If it's not about that, what does it matter?

It matters because whatever I say will look bad.

That's not your problem. Why suffer because of your dad?

Because he's my dad!

But think what he may have done. The FBI doesn't break down doors for nothing.

Sure they do. They make mistakes. Like with Dad's friend, Mr. Ibrahim. He got strip-searched at Newark coming back from the Hajj because of a mix-up with his name.

Who says there was a mix-up? Maybe he just got lucky.

No!

Have it your way. Ibrahim was innocent. They let him

go, didn't they? Your dad'll go free too, if he's clear. Like he says, who needs privacy if there's nothing to hide?

"I won't snitch on Dad!"

It wouldn't be snitching. The FBI knows everything. If they don't, they will. You won't be giving them anything new.

"Stop it! Leave me alone!" Oh god, I said it out loud.

The man swoops in behind me. "If you know something and don't say it, you're toast. Got that? If people die, you'll be an accessory to murder."

"What?"

He squeezes my shoulders hard. "You heard me, Sami. You'll spend the rest of your life in jail."

Save yourself! Save yourself!

The man whirls my chair around. He plants his hands on my arms. Sticks his nose in my face. His breath is hot, pores huge. "You tell me, and you tell me now," he hollers. "Where is Tariq Hasan?"

"Tariq Hasan? Who's Tariq Hasan?"

The man doesn't blink. "Don't play dumb." His head's big and boney, cheeks hollow, hair so cropped he might as well be bald. I should be shaking, but I can't. I'm frozen.

The man relaxes his grip on my arms, grabs the chair behind him, swings it around between his legs, and squats on it. He's older than he looks. I can tell by the veins on the back of his hands, and the tight flap of skin under his chin. One thing's for sure: He's important. Not like the others. No, this one's in a blazer and dress pants.

He leans forward. "I asked you a question, Sami," he says evenly. "Don't make me ask it again. Where is Tariq Hasan?"

"I don't know who you mean. Really." My voice is so light it could float through the ceiling.

The man reaches his arm toward the woman. She hands him a folder. He takes it without looking, pulls out an 8x10, holds it in front of my face.

It's shot from across a street. The guy in the center of the photo is in his early twenties. He's slouched against a wall between a shaded window and a short set of cement steps, wearing a loose, long-sleeved shirt that drops to mid-thigh and matching baggy pants pulled in at the ankle. Oh, and he has a sketchy beard, a skullcap, and a sandal on the foot that's pressed against the brick; and he's smiling. Maybe he's seen a friend. Maybe he's thinking about a joke. Or maybe that's just how he is.

"This is Tariq Hasan?"

"You know him by another name?" the woman asks.

"I don't know him at all."

The man looks right through me. He still hasn't blinked. I'm surprised his eyeballs haven't cracked. If they had, he wouldn't notice. He's the kind of machine who'd do one-armed push-ups on a busted elbow. I wonder if he has a wife. Or kids. I wonder what he'd do if strangers broke into his house in the middle of the night, threw his wife in a room, his son in the basement, and scared the living shit out of them.

He puts the photograph back in the file and pulls out another. "Take another look."

It's a close-up of Hasan's head. He's looking way up, like at something in a window. Or maybe he's just catching some rays. Dark curls sneak out from under the rim of his cap and around his ears. He's still smiling. I wish I had teeth like that; I'd have girlfriends for sure.

"No," I shake my head. "Never seen him."

"Oh?" The way the man says it, I think I've made a mistake. I look at the picture again and again. But I haven't, I really haven't, not ever. Or what if I have, and I don't know it? Like, what if he visited the mosque or something? Or he works at Dad's lab and I saw him in a public area during one of those stupid Take Your Kid to Work days?

I gulp. "I don't think I've seen him, no."

The man rubs his tongue against the back of his teeth, like there's something stuck between his molars. "So you don't *think* you've seen him."

Do I lie? What can I say to make them go away and leave us alone?

"Maybe he's been to the house?" the woman coaxes.

I look over, see her for the first time. Pantsuit. Rings. Flat shoes. Heavy cheeks. A helmet of black, lacquered hair.

"No," I say. "Honest. He's never been here." *Why won't she believe me?* "What's Hasan done?"

"It's not what he's done. It's what he's going to do."

"Which is what?"

The two of them stare at me dead cold.

"Look," I say in a small voice, "*is* this about Toronto?" Nothing. So it is.

I take a deep breath. "Okay, Dad went to a security conference in Toronto. You know that, right? What you don't know is, he was supposed to take me. He bailed because of a woman. I think he's having an affair. But I don't know for sure, I really don't. And anyway, it's between Mom and Dad—it's nobody else's business. Even if it was, Dad has nothing to do with this Tariq Hasan guy, or people getting killed, or anything. He doesn't even know Hasan. I promise. So, like, I think this is all a mistake. Okay?"

The male agent stretches his arms. I get a waft of bad air. He reaches into the file and hands me three more photos.

The top: Hasan again. The smile is gone. There's a storm on his face.

The middle: Hasan's eyes are guarded. He's shaking hands with a man facing away from the camera.

The bottom: The other man's turned around, his expression grim.

It's Dad.

Nineteen

The agents grill me to a crisp. Questions about Dad, his work, who he knows, what he does. I hardly hear a word. My mind's all on that last picture. And I'm saying stuff like, "Dad shakes someone's hand, so what? What's he charged with? What?"

But Cigar Breath and Hairdo, they don't do answers. Just fire off more questions, like rounds at a shooting gallery. Question, question, question—

I'm filled with a sudden terror. What if Mom's been taken away too? When the agents leave, how will I find her? Or Dad?

Or what if—oh my God—a nightmare worse than the worst nightmare ever—

"We're Americans," I blurt out. "Mom and Dad—you can't put them on a plane. You can't send them off to be tortured."

"Answer the question," Cigar Breath yells.

"Which one?"

"The lab. What has your dad brought home from the lab?"

"Nothing. How would I know?"

"You live here. You see things."

"No."

"Tell us!"

"You tell me first: Where's Dad? Where's Mom? What have you done with them?"

And suddenly I can't see or hear or think, and I'm trying to force myself out of the chair, only my legs won't work, nothing works, and I'm helpless, and that's when I realize the questions have stopped, and the woman has her hand on the man's arm, and they're staring at me, waiting for me to quit sobbing, heaving, to calm down, to, to—

"We know you're a good boy, Sami," the woman says. "A good son."

I'm not. I'm not.

"You'd do anything for your father, right?" She watches

me rock back and forth. "He's in serious trouble. The best way to help him is by helping us."

"But I don't know anything," I whisper. "I don't. I . . ." My voice drifts into silence.

The man gets a text on his BlackBerry, texts back, cracks his knuckles and neck. "We're done."

The woman hands me a card: FBI, Squad 9, phone and e-mail. "Your mother's waiting for you upstairs," she says quietly. "If you think of anything unusual about your father's behavior these past few weeks, no matter how small, get in touch."

The agents get me to stand up, and follow me upstairs.

It's like a bomb went off in the kitchen. The drawers are all on the floor, dish towels and cutlery scattered everywhere. The cupboards, stove, and fridge doors are open. All the containers are gone: juice and milk cartons, canned food, spice jars. Why?

Mom's down the hall in the family room. Four agents stand at ease. The carpets are ripped up, the furniture's a jumble. When Mom sees me, she leaps off the ottoman and opens her arms. I try not to run to her, but I do anyway. She holds me.

Maybe the agents mutter something when they leave.

Maybe they don't. All I hear is Mom's heart, and the sound of the sleeve of her housecoat over my ear. Next thing I know, we're alone.

"Are you all right?" she asks.

I shiver a nod.

She puts a mohair blanket around my shoulders, the one she uses when she curls up to read, and sets me down on the sectional.

"You sit tight, while I make a few calls. Don't go near the end of the room. There's glass on the floor."

I glance at the French doors. Somebody's closed the curtains, but I can see the smashed locks on the inside of the frames; the coffee table's been placed across them to keep the doors shut. I have this flash of the break-in.

"Can you call from in here?" I ask, pulling the blanket around me like I'm three years old or something.

Mom strokes my hair. "Don't worry. I'm not going anywhere."

The phone is out of its dock, lying by the door. She picks it up and calls our imam.

It's barely six A.M., but he's already up for predawn prayers. I watch Mom's face as she tells him what's happened. The muscles are tight around her eyes and lips, but her voice is calm. It's the same as that time last winter, when she was driving me home from a day of sledding in the country and we got caught in a whiteout.

"I don't know where they've taken him," Mom says into the phone. Her eyes are locked on the Qur'an, rooted, like if they moved, they'd tear from their sockets.

The Qur'an's the only thing in the room that hasn't been touched. Or maybe it was, and it's the one thing Mom's put back in place. Whatever—it's on its pedestal next to the prayer rug shelves. The rugs are on the floor in a heap, along with Mom's hijab. Our flat-screen TV's propped against them. Everything's off the walls: the art, the sconces, the ceiling lamps, even the switch plates. Everything's away from the walls too, and not just the sectional, chairs, and corner tables. The bookcases on either side of the fireplace have been yanked out, hardcovers and paperbacks torn apart, tossed aside. As for the fireplace, the grill's upside down on the carpet, the fake logs smashed.

What was the FBI looking for? What did they think Dad was hiding? And what's his connection to Hasan?

The imam must be saying something important. Mom's eyes have left the Qur'an. They're darting like finches. Her free arm waves in a circle. "Sami. Paper. Pen."

I scramble for the scratch pad and ballpoint next to the upended corner table. Mom grabs them out of my hand, presses the phone between her ear and shoulder, and scribbles. "Thank you. Thanks so much. I'll be waiting for his call." She hangs up.

"And?" I say.

"The imam's getting us a lawyer." She gestures vaguely at the room. "And someone to make repairs."

"What about Dad?"

"Don't worry. The lawyer'll find out where he is, and when we can get him home."

Out of nowhere, Mom's face goes strange. She reaches out and touches the door frame for balance. It's like she's lost, like she's stepped out of a car crash into a fog.

"Mom?"

The light clicks back in her eyes. "Wait just a sec," she says, and marches upstairs. Next thing I know, she's got out her whisk broom, dust pan, and vacuum.

I give her a look. She tosses it back: "You think this glass is going to disappear by itself?"

I'm not sure what I'm supposed to be doing, but sitting on my butt isn't it. I get up and wander down the hall to the living room. There's some kind of commotion outside. I glance out the bay window.

My stomach lurches.

Our yard is marked off with crime-scene tape. There's a cruiser across the driveway and another by the curb. A couple of cops are keeping people to the opposite side of the street. Mostly it's clusters of neighbors in dressing gowns, holding coffee cups. But there's two camera crews too. I see their vans parked a few doors down, and a third coming up the street.

I turn out the living room light so they can't see inside. Because that's exactly what everyone's trying to do. I wish we had curtains, but no, we're stuck with sheers and this stupid window-treatment thing Mom saw in a magazine.

I press against the side of the bay and peek out. I spot Andy and Marty in hoodies and track pants. Andy's jumping up and down waving his cell.

I race downstairs to find mine; no way I'm going outside to get mobbed. Last I remember, my cell was in my jeans. And they'd be where, exactly? Oh right, in a ball in the corner. My clothes are the one mess the agents had nothing to do with.

I get Andy and Marty right away. "You been up all night?"

"No kidding, dude." Andy's totally wired. "You okay?"

"Fine."

"Is it true about your dad?" from Marty.

"Is what true?"

"Turn on your TV," Andy says.

"My TV?"

"Yeah, you heard me. Pick a channel. Your dad's famous."

"Crazy's more like it," Marty says. "At least the way he looks in the video."

"What video?"

"I think Hutchison took it, the asshole," Andy says.

Hutchison's this crusty gun nut who lives across the street. He's one of the neighbors who tried to stop Mom and Dad from buying here. The Shriners kicked him out for being too embarrassing, but he's still got the go-kart. Every summer, he gets tanked up and races it around the crescent in his idiot Ali Baba costume.

"Hutchison's blabbing his face off," Andy says. "He was getting back from a party when the FBI hauled your dad out. He recorded it on his cell and sold it."

I hear a strange woman's voice in the background. "They say you two are friends with Sabiri's son. Could I talk to you?"

"Reporter," Andy says into the phone. "Don't worry.

We'll put in a good word."

"No! Don't say anything!"

But Andy doesn't hear me. In fact, nobody hears anybody. The whole world's turned into this loud, throbbing whirr.

I know that sound. It's a chopper.

Twenty

The chopper belongs to the local news station. They use it for morning traffic reports. Today there's a major snarl around our subdivision. You know how cars slow down to check out crashes? Well, guess what they do when the FBI arrives on a terror bust?

Mom and I are on the floor, bunched together, backs pressed to the sectional, staring at the TV. It's also on the floor, still propped against the prayer rugs. When I told Mom that Dad was on all the morning news shows, she plugged it into the nearest socket. We've been glued here ever since, trying to find out what's going on.

It's seven thirty in the morning now, and still nobody knows anything for sure. All that's certain is whatever's happening is big. It involves an international terrorist cell in Toronto. And Dad.

Authorities have released photos of twelve guys in their twenties. They're all bearded and scruffy. One of them is Tariq Hasan, looking way less *GQ* than in the FBI's 8x10s. In some shots, the men are in traditional Islamic dress, apparently at various locations around a Toronto public housing project. In others, they're out in the countryside, marching in camouflage through woods and across fields.

We see the grainy video of Dad too, taken from Hutchison's cell phone. The buttons on Dad's pajama top are popped open. His eyes are glassy, hair wild, face contorted. Agents struggle to force him into their van. He looks crazy to kill.

According to unconfirmed reports, the cell calls itself the Brotherhood of Martyrs. Experts can't say if it's a rogue operation or an offshoot of Al Quaeda. Whatever, eleven of its members were arrested by the Royal Canadian Mounted Police in a predawn sweep, coordinated with the FBI's arrest of Dad. A couple are landed residents and refugee claimants, but most are illegals operating on expired student visas or fake passports.

The exception is cell leader Tariq Hasan. A reporter

stands outside a narrow blue door in a wall of storefronts. He says Hasan lived in one of the apartments upstairs. Someone must've tipped him to the raid, because he's escaped without a trace. Authorities say he's armed and extremely dangerous. A woman, face covered by a niqab, pushes past the reporter with a bag of groceries. The reporter yells questions about Hasan. She disappears behind the blue door.

This stuff gets repeated nonstop along with shots of our house, taken from both the traffic helicopter and street-level TV cameras. There's also interviews with our neighbors: "We've never had a terrorist in Meadowvale." "Sabiri, a quiet guy, but strange. Belonged to the golf club, but never played." Those kind of interviews.

Andy and Marty have maybe three seconds of face time per network. Each time, Marty bobs his head like an idiot, while Andy shifts around, hands sunk in his pockets, saying crap like, "Sammy, he's a great guy. Great guy. Yo, hang in there Sammy." Gee thanks, Andy. Let the world know my name, why don't you.

Around seven forty-five, the phone rings. Mom puts it on speaker so I can hear too.

"Hosam Bhanjee, here," the man says. It sounds like he's just woken up. In the background I hear kids complaining about their breakfast cereal. "I just listened to a voice mail from Imam Habib," Mr. Bhanjee says. "I understand your husband needs some legal assistance. I'm booked with other clients all morning, but I'll make time this afternoon. With your husband's background, I expect whatever the problem is will sort itself out fairly quickly."

Mom clears her throat. "Mr. Bhanjee, have you been watching the news?"

"No. Why?"

"Watch the news." She hangs up, closes her eyes.

So do I. Hosam Bhanjee is a lawyer who goes to our mosque. He specializes in immigration hearings, especially since 9/11. He's got a good reputation. But this is *so* beyond anything that's happened around here.

"Mom," I say, trying not to panic, "Mr. Bhanjee's office can find Dad. And Bhanjee has all sorts of contacts, in case he needs, well, special help."

Mom tries to smile, but the TV snaps out a drum roll. It's a Breaking News Alert.

The news anchor's face is stern: "According to our inside sources, alleged terrorist Dr. Arman Sabiri is research director at Shelton Laboratories. The lab, a category-four facility outside Rochester, stores anthrax, smallpox, and other viruses and microtoxins. For viewers joining us, Dr. Sabiri is reputed to be the American link to the Brotherhood of Martyrs, an alleged terrorist cell based in Toronto, Canada."

We see live footage from outside the lab. Police, firemen, and paramedics are on standby. Men in white sci-fi bodysuits are entering the doorway. Clusters of people are being herded into trailers.

"Workers at Shelton are being interviewed by law enforcement agents," the anchor continues. "The lab will be on lockdown, pending an audit of all bio-units, canisters, and other containers. Off the record, authorities confirm that the Brotherhood is believed to have planned cross-border biological attacks targeting mass transportation and food and water supplies."

The phone rings. Mom answers. "Hello?"

"Is this the Sabiri residence?" a pleasant male voice asks over the speakers.

"Yes," Mom says. "Are you Mr. Bhanjee's assistant?"

The voice goes twisted: "Your family's going to die, whore dog, pig fuck!" Then it starts screaming obscenities about the Prophet and Islam.

Mom freezes.

"Look asshole," I yell at the phone, "our phone line is

bugged. Got it? That means you're on record. Do anything to us, you're busted!"

The phone goes dead.

Mom looks at me in wonder. I shrug.

But there's no time to worry about obscene phone calls. Science types are popping up on all the channels, discussing Dad and bioterrorism. Like, which organisms he worked with are airborne or waterborne. And which viruses can infect a handful of innocent people on subways, buses, and planes, who can then infect hundreds more before they show symptoms—at which point those hundreds have infected thousands, who've infected tens of thousands, and on and on. They talk about swine flu and bird flu, and how in an age of air travel, pandemics can sweep around the world in days, killing us all before we know it.

Five minutes of this, I'm afraid to go outside. The anchors say that talk of a biological strike is still speculation. "But with Hasan on the loose, authorities are scrambling to discover what he's received from Dr. Sabiri." It's like, Good morning, America. You're going to die, but don't panic.

Networks go to a live feed from Toronto, where Canadian police are showing off a room full of evidence they collected in their raids. There's tables of drugs, fake passports, and weapons—guns, rifles, ammo, machetes—plus camouflage gear, a door with bullet holes, and five shot-up mannequins. Worse, there's marked plastic bags with batteries, phones, cameras, wire cutters, electrical devices—and five lead-lined boxes supposedly filled with sealed containers of unidentified powders. How it all fits, the authorities don't say, but it's scary.

By now, our phone's ringing every few minutes. None of the callers are listed. Who cares? We're not answering anyway. After the first crank, Mom called Mr. Bhanjee's law office to light a fire under his butt. It was already lit. He'd turned on the news, dropped his morning clients, and been working to find Dad ever since. "The case is more complicated than I'd anticipated," he said. Jump to the head of the class, Brainiac.

Andy and Marty try to phone me, but I turn off my cell. I just want to be quiet with Mom. I look at her face. She's thinking the same as me: Where's Dad? What are they doing to him? Why was he in that photo with Hasan?

At ten A.M., the networks go on standby for a Homeland Security press briefing in Washington. There's shots of government buildings and limos and people with security badges talking into headsets.

All of a sudden the news cuts to a media room. A man with a buzz cut and a dark suit is standing behind a podium. Behind him, a row of other men in buzz cuts and dark suits, like copies off a printer.

The man keeps it short. He confirms the detentions, and the escape of cell leader Tariq Hasan. "These detentions follow an international surveillance investigation, code-named Operation Patriot Action. The investigation targeted the Brotherhood of Martyrs and Dr. Arman Sabiri. Dr. Sabiri is a research director at Shelton Laboratories, the category-four bio lab near Rochester, New York."

Blah, blah, blah. Then a bombshell:

"E-mail correspondence and cell phone records between Brotherhood leader Tariq Hasan and Dr. Sabiri reveal that Dr. Sabiri was about to provide Hasan with secret materials. These materials are classified information."

Classified. Right. Dad's director of a lab with live anthrax, smallpox, viruses, and microtoxins. Figure it out.

"The FBI and Homeland Security, in cooperation with Canada's Royal Canadian Mounted Police, and the Canadian Security Intelligence Service, conducted their early morning raids the day before Dr. Sabiri was scheduled to make the drop-off at a motel on the outskirts of Rochester."

An explosion of flashbulbs. The man puts up his hand for order.

"The Brotherhood of Martyrs is now in custody. It is no longer a threat. However, cell leader Tariq Hasan remains at large. He is considered armed and extremely dangerous. Until his capture, the country remains at Orange Alert. We urge the public to remain calm. Thank you."

The man steps back from the podium. He turns to the exit.

Reporters wave microphones. "Tariq Hasan! Have you found Tariq Hasan?" "Do you know where Hasan is hiding?" "What were his plans?" "Do you know what he's got?"

"No questions," the man says. "No comment." He heads out the door.

Shouts from the reporters. Alarmed news analysis from the TV anchors.

Dad. What have you done?

Twenty-one

Two minutes later, there's a report that members of the Brotherhood of Martyrs are being detained at Toronto's Don Jail on security certificates. Dad's being held at the Rochester Correctional Facility, a state prison not far from here. There's no word on charges. That doesn't stop the networks from posting a video still of Dad's deranged face under the headline: DR. DEATH?

I head upstairs to the linen closet. Sheets, blankets, towels, and pillowcases are strewn along the hallway; the floor looks like a miniature Thousand Islands made out of cotton and wool. I untangle a few blankets, haul them to the living room, and step up on a chair so I can hang them over the rod above the bay window.

"Sami, get down off your father's chair," Mom calls from down the hall in the family room. She's watching my drapery antics on TV. I give the finger to whatever camera crew is filming me. "Sami!" Mom explodes.

TV aerial shots have made the street look like a parking lot. At ground level, it's even more jammed. Moms with strollers, kids playing hooky, and people who've detoured in from Oxford Drive—they've all decided our little crescent is a tourist spot. The Robinson twins from two doors down have even set up a lemonade stand.

No sign of Andy and Marty, though. I turn on my cell. They've left a gazillion messages. I call right away. They're freaking out in Andy's basement. After they went on TV, the FBI agents took them to a van and questioned them about being my friends and if they'd heard me talk about stuff.

"We said no," Andy volunteers.

"What else did you say?"

"Nothing."

"Bullshit."

"Okay," he confesses, "just that your dad's real strict, he's always praying, and a joke about the Prophet'll send him off his nut. Anyway, they took our addresses and phone numbers. Shit, man, cops at the door are one thing, but if our folks find out the FBI's on our case, they'll kill us."

"Right, so shut up, if you know what's good for you," Marty hisses at Andy. "The agents said the interview was classified. We shouldn't be telling him anything."

"'*Him*'?"

"No offense," Andy says, "but Marty's right. We shouldn't talk."

"Suit yourself, dickhead!" I hang up, hoping they'll call back to say they're sorry. They don't.

There's a knock on the front door. I peek between my makeshift curtains. It's a couple of installers from Akmed Windows and Doors: at least, that's the name on their van. I hope Akmed appreciates the publicity.

Mom's not trusting anyone. Before she'll talk to them, she makes them go around to the backyard and give her our imam's name. Turns out they're legit. They measure the French doors and say it'll be Monday before they can get replacements. In the meantime, they bolt sheets of plywood over the busted frames. At noon, they break for Juma prayers. That's when I notice the paparazzi in the golf club's trees. Just what we need: Shots Of The Door Guys bowing to Mecca in our little backyard war zone.

I point the paparazzi out to Mom. "You should fire a

few line drives at 'em with your three wood."

"Right." Mom nods grimly. "Maybe wear a burka while I'm at it. Give the sons of bitches their money's worth."

I'm so shocked, I laugh.

Mom's eyes mist. "What would I do without you?"

I look away, cuz I'm thinking the same about her.

The door guys leave as Eddy Harrison's crew shows up on lunch break. What with the crowd filling the street, Eddy parks the right side of his BMW on Mr. Hutchison's front lawn. He and his friends get out of the car and start feeding their faces with burgers, fries, and jumbo Cokes. Hutchison stands on his porch and swears at them. Eddy just laughs and tosses his food wrappers in Hutchison's bushes. Next thing you know, Hutchison's soaking Eddy and his gang with a high-power garden hose. Eddy goes apeshit, but the cops step in fast. The gang disappears.

Nothing new happens till four. That's when Mr. Bhanjee phones to say he's still trying to see Dad. He promises he'll be over right after. "Right after" turns out to be nine o'clock. Mom and I watch for him through the window blankets in our darkened living room. Outside, it's bright as day from all the camera crews, cars, and vans.

A police escort guides Mr. Bhanjee's Mazda to our

roped-off driveway. He's swarmed by press. As he backs toward our door, answering questions, he pats the air like he's taming lions at the circus. Lucky for him, he's on our side of the police tape, or he'd be eaten alive.

We lead him back to the family room. Mr. Bhanjee settles onto the sectional and wipes a hand over well-gelled hair. He's had a hard, sweaty day. He keeps his jacket on out of respect for Mom, but it's unbuttoned and his shirt's so damp you can see his undershirt. You don't want to. Mr. Bhanjee's one of those totally hairy guys who have to shave a crescent between their beard and chest so they won't look like the Wolfman. He's also waxed a gap in his unibrow.

Mom offers him tea.

Mr. Bhanjee adds four lumps of sugar, but passes on Mom's ginger snaps because, apparently, he's on a diet. He holds his cup and saucer under his chin. "I've spoken to Arman. He says to tell you both he loves you. And he's innocent."

Mom presses her hands on her knees. "How is he?" she asks softly.

Mr. Bhanjee raises his shoulders as if to say, how do you think? "It's hard to know. I saw him less than five minutes. He was behind glass. There were guards."

Mom's on her feet. "If he's being questioned, he has a right to a lawyer! Why weren't you there? Why *aren't* you there?"

Mr. Bhanjee sets his tea on the coffee table, adjusts the crease of his pants at the knee, and folds his hands. I focus on his lips, his mouth spilling words that make the air so thick I can't breathe: "Mrs. Sabiri, there's the law—and there's the law. In the case of an imminent terror attack, the government justifies violations of individual rights."

"But Arman might say things that can be twisted against him later!"

Mr. Bhanjee shakes his head. "Prosecutors can't use statements made without a lawyer present. That's why I doubt they're asking him questions about himself."

"They want him to lead them to Hasan," I whisper.

Mr. Bhanjee lifts the left half of his giant eyebrow. "That's my guess, yes."

Mom sits down again; squeezes the sides of the ottoman. "So what do we do now?"

"Courts are closed for the weekend, and your husband's under tight security," Mr. Bhanjee says. "Monday morning I can fight for his release. He's being held in preventive detention as a material witness. But so far, he hasn't been charged."

"What are your odds of getting him out?"

Mr. Bhanjee taps his lips with his napkin. "As you can understand, with terror threats, judges are reluctant to second-guess the government. Suppose someone with information about an attack is released and a strike follows. Imagine the outrage. Not to mention the consequences to the judge. They're elected, don't forget. Political rule number one: Avoid risk."

Mom hesitates: "So how long could Arman be held?"

"Only God knows."

Mom leans forward. "Mr. Bhanjee, I know things look bad, but I also know my husband. This thing is a mistake. All day we've heard 'unconfirmed reports' and 'off-the-record sources.' But where's the evidence? Why do they think Arman's involved?"

Mr. Bhanjee opens and closes his hands. "If a terrorist threat is believed to exist, evidence is kept secret. National security. When I apply for your husband's release, the government will give the judge a summary of its case. Any names, or details that could reveal those names, will be redacted."

"Redacted?"

"Edited out. It's to protect the lives of informants. And to prevent terrorists from using the information to regroup."

"So anyone can say anything, and we have no idea who's saying what," Mom exclaims.

I start to sweat. "Without names and details, fighting for Dad will be like wrestling fog."

"I'm afraid that's right." Mr. Bhanjee nods. "And there's something else to understand: There are risks even if I win your father's release."

Mom and I look at each other, bewildered, then at Mr. Bhanjee.

"Right now," Mr. Bhanjee explains, "Arman's only being held as a witness. But if a judge sets him free, the government can decide to lay charges—any charges—to keep him in jail. Once he's charged, proving his innocence can take years and cost a fortune."

Mom freezes. "Our home. Sami's education. We could end up on the street."

"You can use a public defender," Mr. Bhanjee says, "but their resources are limited."

Mom waves her hand. "Forget the future. We have to make it through the now." She tries to get up. She can't. She grips her knees. "My husband's lived here for more than twenty years. He's a loyal American."

"Loyal or not," Mr. Bhanjee says, "if he's found guilty, his citizenship will be stripped. He can be deported to where he was born."

"Iran!" Mom gasps. "But he fled Iran! If he's sent back, think what they'll do!"

"There's one hope," Mr. Bhanjee says. "If I'm right, this terror threat caught officials off guard. Despite the detentions, no charges have been laid on either side of the border."

"You think the authorities are simply fishing?" Mom asks. "Holding suspects while they investigate?"

"It's possible," Mr. Bhanjee says. "If so, the apparent terror threat may turn out to be nothing. Or nothing as it relates to your husband."

Mom closes her eyes. "Then let's pray that's all it is. Nothing, Mashallah. And that when the government sees that, Mashallah, all will be well, Mashallah."

Mr. Bhanjee studies his hands. I watch him rub his left thumb against the meat of his right palm. Something's bothering him—and me too. I think of the FBI, the crowds, the press, the networks.

"Mr. Bhanjee," I say, "a lot of time and energy's gone into making Dad look like a terrorist. If it turns out he isn't, some very important people are going to look stupid. Nobody likes to look stupid. Not at home. Not at school. Not anywhere."

Mr. Bhanjee sees me hesitate. "Go on."

I swallow hard. "So . . . suppose the evidence against Dad turns out to be nothing. Or suppose stuff shows up that proves he's innocent. As long as that stuff is secret, there'll be people who'll want to *keep* it secret. Important people—people with power. In that case, the truth won't ever get out. Dad will never be able to clear his name."

Mr. Bhanjee turns to Mom. "You have a very smart son."

Twenty-two

Mom and I stay inside for the weekend.

The news—and I mean *all* the news—is still about Dad. You'd think nothing else was happening in the world. It's not like they have much to add, either. It's just the same old clips of Dad looking crazy as he's dragged away, the FBI sweep of Shelton Laboratories, and photos of the Brotherhood of Martyrs.

Well, okay, there's some new stuff. Canada's RCMP has released a few videos the Brotherhood took of their training exercises. There's shots of them firing off rounds in some farm field, and Tariq Hasan laughing about how they should take out the prime minister of Canada and his parliament too. And on CNN there's a segment with a

Rochester reporter that comes with footage of the Akmed door guys praying behind our house; an interview with Mom's boss at the drug store; and, truly embarrassing, news that "Sabiri's son, Mohammed, is a student at the exclusive Theodore Roosevelt Academy." Like, what's the point? Terrorists educate their kids?

I have a flash of Dad enrolling me. I remember thinking I was in prison. But that's nothing like what he's going through now. I wonder how he is. The not knowing drives me crazy.

I phone Andy and Marty. They don't pick up or return my texts. In fact, the only calls I get have unidentified caller ID. Cranks. How did they get my number? From someone at school? Eddy? How did he find it? Who cares? I delete them all, without bothering to listen.

Andy and Marty. Why did I have to hang up mad? I want to talk to them. I need to. Don't they know that? Maybe they're scared because of the FBI. Or maybe their folks have said not to talk to me. I mean, who knows who's being bugged by now?

All the same, them cutting me off, it hurts. I want to bang on Andy's door and make him tell me what's happening. But there's still camera people around to record us. And I'm afraid of what he might say. As long as I don't know, I can pretend the silence doesn't mean anything. But if he says we can't be friends anymore, I don't know what I'll do.

I try not to think about it. Saturday, I help Mom clean up. Sunday, I help her play host to visitors from the mosque. Mom's prepared tea and food for everyone, but the women have brought groceries and serving trays of their own. All afternoon, they work in the kitchen so Mom won't have to think about cooking meals till, like, forever.

Me, I'm sent to the family room with the men. They shake my hand, double-hug me, and pat my back. This is to give me strength for "the difficult days ahead." Seeing as Dad's in jail, I'm supposedly the Man Of The House. Whatever that means. I suck it up and try to look tough, or however a Man Of The House is supposed to look. Not like an awkward geek anyway, which is how I feel. It'd be easier if I had a beard.

Imam Habib is seated in the recliner at the end of the room, in front of the plywood over the French doors. He rises to give a brief talk. His eyes are watery. I wonder if it's because of cataracts, like with Marty's grandma. His voice is old too. There's a little rattle at the end of his sentences, like his lungs aren't so good. It doesn't matter.

He's gentle without being a wimp, and knows all the right things to say. Mostly he talks about how this is a time of testing but we'll come out of the fire stronger, like steel; and how the prophet Musa—Moses—spent forty years in the wilderness, but God was with him.

The imam's words are comforting for most of us. But they're not enough for Mr. Ibrahim. He's never forgotten his strip search in Newark. "When Timothy McVeigh bombed the Oklahoma City building, the government didn't round up blond-haired, blue-eyed Christians!" he shouts. "When the IRA bombed London, the West didn't declare war on Catholics!"

I put a finger to my lips and point to the holes in the walls. There could be listening devices anywhere. Everything that's been said in private could be recorded. Probably is. For sure, everyone who's come through the door has been photographed.

Mr. Ibrahim settles himself with a cigarette. Considering the plywood over the French doors has turned the room into a tomb, I'm ticked. But if I say anything about smoking being haraam, I'll put Imam Habib on the spot, which'll make me a bad host, so I shut up, and pray that Mom's stocked up on air freshener.

She has. Incense, anyway. After evening prayers,

when everyone finally leaves, she lights four sticks of sandalwood, sets one at each corner of the room, and burrows into the corner of the sectional with *Golf Digest*. I leave her alone, heading off for some quiet time of my own.

I try downstairs, but my room feels empty without my computer. The living room's weird too, with the blankets over the windows to shut out the clusters of people who're still outside. Apparently, they haven't figured out the show's over, and they should maybe get a life.

Where I end up is in Dad's office. It's the one room in the house Mom and I left untouched when we cleaned up. I've hardly ever been in here: that time a few weeks back when I got into his computer; the time after Mary Louise, when he gave me an online tour of the Academy; and a few times when I was little. I mean, this is Dad's room. The room you only go into if you want to die.

I leave the lights off. The dusk is all I need.

Dad's carpets are heaved up and over. The family portraits and Dad's degrees are knocked off the walls. His desk's pulled forward, all its drawers missing. The computer, printer, scanner, and filing cabinets are gone too. His roll-chair is in the corner, the leather ripped open; ditto the cushions on the window seat.

I don't know why, but I have this weird need to snuggle into the empty space under his desk; it looks so safe and secure, like my cubbyhole at the Academy. I crawl under and curl up, arms around my knees, in the place where his feet would be. Dad. I imagine his hands on a keyboard over my head. I imagine him humming, or chanting a favorite verse from the Qur'an. Dad.

When I was in middle school, there was a kid who dropped dead in the middle of a volleyball game. Drew Lazar. Twelve years old, and he just dropped dead. His brother says their mom's kept Drew's room the way it was the day he died. The old posters are still up. The bed's unmade. There's a sneaker on the desk. He says the room is cold.

It's like that here, now. This cold. This strange cold. Like Dad's gone and he's never coming back. And this room will stay exactly the same, the way it was the night he left and our world changed, forever.

In the near-dark, Dad smiles at me from the small framed photo of him and me—the one where I'm maybe six and his beard is tickling my cheek. It's on the floor now, across the room. It must've been knocked off the desk and kicked aside during the raid. Somehow it's landed upright, propped against an overturned wastebasket.

The glass over the picture has broken into five pieces, but the metal frame is still keeping everything together.

I want to reach out, to take it, to hold it close. But I'm afraid to touch it. What if the shards of glass dislodge and slice the photo? Still, if I leave it lying on the floor, sooner or later it'll get wrecked for sure. I crawl over, carefully cup my hands under the frame, and bring the picture to my room, setting it on the table by my bed.

I rest my head on my pillow and stare at it. Dad. What's the truth, Dad? Did you do something wrong? If you didn't, why are they holding you? Why are they saying those things on TV?

What's going to happen to us?

Twenty-three

All night I have nightmares.

In the last one, I'm in an underground mine. It's pitch black. Mom and Dad are with me. There's dynamite going off. If we don't get out, we'll be buried alive. We race down narrow corridors, feeling the walls with our hands. An explosion. Rocks crash. "Sami!" Dad's under the rubble. I scramble to free him. "Sami!" His voice is far away. The more I dig, the farther it gets. And where's Mom? Another explosion. The floor gives way. I'm falling. Help!

"The devil finds work for idle hands." That's what Mom tells me Monday morning.

My suspension's over, but I was hoping to stay home from school a while longer. I'm afraid of what'll happen when I go back.

"Nothing will happen," Mom says. "Just hold your head high and carry on."

Easy for her to say. She's taken off work to wait for word from Mr. Bhanjee. If he gets Dad a hearing, she'll call the Academy and take me with her to the courthouse.

All the same, even Mom knows it's not business as usual. She drives me to school early, for fear reporters will hassle me if I'm alone on my bike. There's only a few of them outside now, plus a couple of skinny losers with bad tattoos and fancy cameras: freelance paparazzi for the tabloids. I hold my knapsack over my face at the end of the driveway, as they flash through the car windows. Two or three days and they'll be gone, I hope, along with the police tape.

Mom drops me off at the main entrance to the Academy. I glance at the statue of Teddy Roosevelt. I wish I had balls like the ones on his horse. Oh well. I bound up the steps to the doors, concentrating like crazy so I don't trip.

I'm not sure what I was expecting, but this isn't it. I mean, usually it feels like everyone's staring at me, but they really aren't. Today it's like nobody's staring at me, but they really *are*. All down the hall, students are hanging out at their lockers, bragging about their weekends. But the minute they see me, they go quiet and stare at their gym bags. I pass, and it's whistles and talk again.

The entire day is like this. At least I manage to avoid Eddy Duh Turd. Until last period, that is.

I take my seat in Mr. Bernstein's class. I'm the first one there. He nods at me, all friendly, his smile so normal it's bizarre. Does he think I don't know that he knows about Dad? That he's just landed from Mars or something? The giveaway is, he doesn't say anything. Cuz, what *can* he say? How was your weekend, Sami?

The class spills into the room. It's like in the halls: Idiot Central till they see me, then they act like they're in chapel. Except for Eddy. On his way past, he mouths "Osama" and gives me a creepy wink.

Mr. Bernstein revs into gear. "We've spent the last week and a half discussing the Cold War, yes? On the one hand, our very real need to guard against dangers at home and abroad. But on the other, our equally real need to remember what happens to freedom when we cross the border into the land of fear." And he leaps into a riff about other examples: the attacks on the labor movements of the early 1900s, the spying campaign against African-American leaders before the Civil Rights Act, and the internment of Japanese-Americans during World War II.

Out of nowhere he stops and grins. "Your turn."

Silence.

Hunh? Normally there's questions. Arguments. Ideas bouncing back and forth like balls at a ping-pong tournament. Not today.

"Come on," Mr. Bernstein smiles. "I hope I said *something* to offend you." More silence. "Really? You accept everything I say? Nothing to challenge? Oh please. There's always something to challenge. Something to get excited about."

Everyone stares at their desks, like they know something's up. Then Eddy raises his hand. Not excited or anything. Just casual, almost bored. Mr. Bernstein waits a bit to make sure he's not just stretching.

"Mr. Harrison," he says. "How can I help you?"

Eddy curls the corner of his lips. "Well, *sir*, we get why you go on about minorities and all. But what if a minority *needs* watching? What if it's a deadly enemy?"

"Once upon a time," Mr. Bernstein says, "every group I've mentioned was thought to be an enemy that needed watching."

"But today is different, isn't it, *sir*?" He says it cold, like a statement. "If you have a cancer, you don't pretend it doesn't exist, do you, *sir*? No. You cut it out."

The room goes dead. I grip a pencil, keep my head down.

"We remove individuals, Mr. Harrison," Mr. Bernstein says calmly. "Not groups."

"Even when those groups are full of terrorists?" Eddy taunts.

Die, die, why can't I die?

Mr. Bernstein leans against his desk. "The Holocaust was so indescribably evil, it represents the worst terrorism the world can imagine," he says. "Nonetheless, we blame the Nazis for its horrors, not the entire German population."

"With all due respect, *sir*, that was then. There. I'm talking here. Now. There's terrorists in Meadowvale. One got arrested Friday."

"An alleged terrorist," Mr. Bernstein interrupts.

"Yeah, well, we're lucky to be alive. I say we round 'em up and send 'em back where they came from."

I whirl around. "I was born here, Eddy, same as you."

Mr. Bernstein leaps up. "Boys. Let's keep the personal out of this."

"How?" I say. "How???"

Eddy grins, his face a bubble of pus-joy. He's got me.

But Mr. Bernstein throws a curve. "We've had terrorists in this country before," he says, his voice edgy as razors. "Ever heard of the Ku Klux Klan? It lynched African-Americans and torched their communities. It murdered Jews too, and attacked Catholics, homosexuals, and immigrants." Mr. Bernstein's voice pitches higher. "By the early nineteen-twenties, its members included fifteen percent of all adult, white, Protestant males, including society leaders, several governors, and judges. And it had at least one very sympathetic president." He pauses. "Today white supremacists thrive in violent, underground militias. That's here! That's now!" A beat, and he swoops in for the kill. "Tell me, Mr. Harrison, what would you say if your father was treated like a terrorist, simply for being a white, Christian male?"

An ugly smile rolls across Eddy's face. "Are you saying my father's a white supremacist, *sir*? Are you calling him a Nazi terrorist?"

"No," Mr. Bernstein snaps. "I'm saying that we condemn the bloody terrorism of white supremacists, but not the entire ethnic and religious group from which they come."

Mr. Bernstein and Eddy eyeball each other. Neither backs off.

"I want each of you to write a short essay for discussion," Mr. Bernstein says to the class. "Where should we draw the line between liberty and security? When, if ever, should we give up our rights?"

Eddy pulls out his laptop; it's his excuse to look away.

Mr. Bernstein sits behind his desk. He watches us for a while, then opens a file folder full of paperwork.

Suddenly . . .

Rata-tata-tata-tata-tata-tata-tata!

We leap from our desks. Somebody's tossed a string of firecrackers into the middle aisle.

Mr. Bernstein's eyes blaze at Eddy. "Who did this?"

Nobody says anything. Like me, they didn't see. Or they're too scared to say.

Twenty-four

Next morning Mom gets a call from Mr. Bhanjee. Dad has a hearing in the late afternoon. She calls the Academy and arranges to pick me up at noon. Vice Principal McGregor is waiting when she arrives. He brings us to the principal's office.

Mr. Samuels, the principal, has a shock of glossy black hair with a white streak running down the center. He looks like somebody put a skunk on his head. Aside from school assemblies and commencement, you never see him. He's always behind closed doors, dealing with board members and alumni. And Head Secretary Mona James. There's a rumor they're having an affair. "That's why she's called his *head* secretary, get it?" guys snigger. Then they go, "Oh *Mo*na, *Mo*na," and everyone cracks up.

Anyway, Mr. Samuels leaves the day-to-day dirty work to Mr. McGregor, so for him to want a chat means something big is up.

"Delighted to see you, Mr. Samuels," Mom says warily. He goes to shake hands. Mom steps back, touches her right palm to her heart, and bows slightly. "We're expected downtown. I'm afraid there's no time to talk."

"I understand," Mr. Samuels says, as slick as his hair. "I'd just like to express the deep concern the Academy has for you and yours. In difficult times, the last thing a family needs is financial pressure. As a rule, Academy fees are nonrefundable. However, understanding your difficult situation, the board has decided to offer a full refund of Sami's tuition should he choose to withdraw from our program."

"That won't be necessary," Mom says stiffly. "Sami's education is our first priority."

"With respect," Mr. Samuels continues, "considering all that's going on, Sami may find life at the Academy stressful. Homeschooling is an option you might like to consider."

Mom looks him straight in the eye. "So you're concerned about our family's connection to the Academy."

"No, nothing like that," Mr. Samuels says, temples red.

"And I'm sure you're not worried about fund-raising, either. Or having the other parents withdraw their sons."

Mr. Samuels blinks like a pithed frog.

"Know this," Mom says evenly. "My son's fees are paid in full. He has as much right to be here as anyone. And I won't have him punished because of baseless rumors against his father. Is that understood?"

And I follow my mother out of the principal's office, trying to keep my head as high as hers. I hate the Academy. But I'm damned if I'm going to leave now.

We meet Mr. Bhanjee at a Starbucks, a block from the Rochester courthouse.

"This is a 'probable cause' hearing," Mr. Bhanjee tells us, wolfing down a date square. So much for his diet. "The government needs to convince the judge why Arman should be held."

"If they can't, will Dad go free?" I ask.

Mr. Bhanjee gulps the last of his coffee. "That's the hope. But remember, the judge will be cautious. At least we'll get a sense of the nature and size of the problem." He pushes back from the table. We head out.

The streets all around are barricaded to traffic. A wall of police is lined up on the courthouse steps; men with security badges march around, looking important; a government helicopter hovers overhead. Mr. Bhanjee points to nearby rooftops. There's paramilitary types in helmets and flak jackets manning submachine guns. What, they think Al Quaeda's gonna storm downtown Rochester to liberate Dad? Gimme a break.

"Perfect photo op for the cameras," Mr. Bhanjee says.

I can barely hear him over the drone of the chopper. "Hunh?"

"Great way to start the government's case," he shouts.

The media are clustered at the blockade by the main entrance. Mr. Bhanjee elbows a path through. I keep my head buried in my chest, my hoodie up, my arm around Mom. Mr. Bhanjee flashes a pass at the guards, and we're waved in.

I've never been in a courthouse before, so I'm not sure if it's normal for there to be two sets of metal detectors to walk through, at the main doors and again at the entrance to the hearing room. But I can't believe everybody has to have sniffer dogs all over them. This is even worse than when we're at the airport and security bozos rummage through our stuff like we're gonna blow the place up.

Most of the seats are taken by reporters. Mom and I are directed to the bench right behind the defense table. Mr. Bhanjee says there won't be much time to talk to Dad, and we shouldn't say much anyway, because who knows what someone might hear and how they might report it.

Dad's brought through a side door, a guard on either side. He's in prison uniform, handcuffed and shackled at the ankles. I want to run to him. He sees me. For a second, a cloud rolls off his face. Then he hangs his head in shame.

They put him behind Mr. Bhanjee's table, right in front of us.

"Dad, I miss you," I whisper.

He nods like he's heard, but he doesn't turn around. Mom reaches forward and touches him gently on the arm. His head and shoulders shake.

Mr. Bhanjee passes a tissue to Dad and whispers to him. Dad stays in control, but I can tell he's upset; his head bobs, like he's a bird pecking the ground for seeds.

The clerk says, "All rise," like in the movies, and we do. "Court is in session. The honorable Judge Chapman presiding."

The judge swings in on crutches. His head's this old apple, wizened and red and covered in brown spots.

Mr. Bhanjee starts by complaining about Dad's handcuffs and shackles. The judge agrees, and orders them removed. Point for our side.

Then Mr. Bhanjee says, "Your Honor, Dr. Sabiri is being held as a material witness. A witness to what? To date, no charges of any kind have been filed relating to my client. We ask for his immediate release."

Before the judge can blink, the lead prosecutor's on his feet. With his bald head and boney hands, he looks like a skeleton in a suit.

"Your Honor," the prosecutor starts, and then he's off and running about Dad and the Brotherhood of Martyrs. He uses PowerPoint to introduce the militia videos we've all seen on TV, and the photographs the FBI shoved in my face of Dad meeting Tariq Hasan weeks ago during his trip to Toronto.

Then he shows the court something new: The e-mail Dad sent to Hasan the day before the raid. He reads it aloud:

> There must be nothing further to connect us. No more letters, calls, or e-mails. Be at the Best Western by the Rochester airport on Friday. I'll pick you up midafternoon to show you around the area, but I can't get you into the lab.

Your trip will be rewarding. Getting the items you wanted out of storage was difficult. Not sure how I'd have explained it, if I was caught. Never mind. They're packed and ready for you to take back to Toronto.

Tariq, I admire your plans. I pray for your success, Inshallah.

Dad shrivels in his seat. He turns to Mom and me: "It's not what it looks like." *No? Then what is it, Dad?* "I've told them. They won't believe me." *Wonder why?*

I lower my head. I can't even look at him.

But Mr. Bhanjee is tough. He flicks his hand at the screen: "That e-mail proves nothing."

"Oh?" the prosecutor says. "Then perhaps my learnèd friend can explain how Dr. Sabiri, a middle-aged director of a category-four bio lab, happens to know Tariq Hasan, a young, unemployed Canadian and head of the Brotherhood of Martyrs. Perhaps he can explain Hasan's plans, what items Dr. Sabiri was going to give him, and where those items are now."

"My client doesn't have to explain anything," Mr. Bhanjee retorts.

The prosecutor stares right through him. "Your Honor," he says, "Tariq Hasan is an imminent threat. He remains at large. It is reasonable to believe that Dr. Sabiri has information regarding his whereabouts."

Mr. Bhanjee objects. The judge overrules him.

The prosecutor raises himself to full height. "Your Honor, Homeland Security is currently on the lookout for an additional conspirator linked to the Brotherhood. A conspirator active in the Rochester area. A conspirator who may, even now, be in possession of biological weapons."

Pandemonium.

"Order," Judge Chapman bangs his gavel. "Order!"

"Dr. Sabiri is the link between the Brotherhood and these biological weapons," the prosecutor thunders. "We believe he knows the identity and whereabouts of the secret conspirator." He gives the judge a file marked Classified. "Until Hasan and this mystery terrorist are located and captured, public security demands that Dr. Sabiri remain in custody."

Twenty-five

They keep Dad in jail.

Mr. Bhanjee tells us to hang tough. "Things look bad, but the evidence is weak. A single e-mail. And no mention of dangerous substances or any public threat. I'll be filing papers immediately, demanding to see evidence of this so-called 'new, unidentified terrorist.'"

Dad's e-mail and the mystery terrorist: that's the big news on TV. There's speculation about who the terrorist might be. One of Dad's co-workers? Someone from our mosque? There's an interview with a criminal profiler. He says the secret conspirator is likely "an unemployed male with low self-esteem." On the other hand, he could be "a high achiever." A reporter suggests "he" could even be a woman, noting the female suicide bombers in Iraq and Afghanistan.

"Great," Mom says bitterly. "The suspect is anybody brown."

If the weekend was bad, the rest of today is hell.

Mr. Bhanjee says not to jump to conclusions: "There's nothing to tie this unidentified terrorist to your father."

Mom nods her head.

Are they blind? Dad and another suspect from the Rochester area are linked to the same foreign terrorist cell. And they don't know each other? What are the odds?

"I'm not going to school tomorrow," I say, as another image of Dr. Death, a.k.a. Dad, flashes on the screen.

"Oh yes, you are," Mom says. "All of them out there, they're waiting to see us crack. Well we won't. We're Sabiris. We stick together no matter what."

"Mom! Think what he tried to do!"

She slaps me. I stare at her in shock. A look of horror crosses her face. She hugs me close. "Forgive me. But your father needs our strength. We musn't betray him."

"Like, he hasn't betrayed us?" I whisper. "Like, he hasn't betrayed our country?"

A long pause. "We don't know that. All we know is, your father is your father."

* * *

It's the middle of the night.

I'm staring at that framed photo on my bedside table, the one of me and Dad from his office. Who *is* he? Who is he really? I don't know. I don't care. I hate him. He's ruined my life. Mom's too.

I go to throw it in the garbage. But I can't.

Dad.

I remember the time I had whooping cough. I thought my lungs were going to rip themselves inside out. I thought I was going to die. Dad stayed by my side day and night for a week, rocking me and singing me Persian lullabies, not caring if he got sick. Just willing me to be well.

Or there was the time before I met Andy and Marty, when I was little and all alone. I remember how one day he found me crying, and he held me and told me how his granny smuggled him out of Iran, how he came to North America without family or friends, how he was so scared he wanted to die, how he met Mom and had me and then everything got better. "You'll get through this," he said. "I promise." And I burrowed my head into his chest, and for a while I didn't mind not having friends, because I had him and Mom, and nothing else mattered.

Mom's right. Dad wouldn't do what they say he's

done. There's got to be another explanation. Maybe Hasan pretended to be a scientist working on a project, or a conference delegate—the leader of a terror cell could easily forge credentials. Maybe Dad was giving Hasan secret research reports, thinking he was legit.

Then why did he want to break off contact? Why was he scared to get caught taking "the items" out of storage?

Because—because maybe Hasan claimed to be a bio-lab inspector. Maybe Dad was acting as a whistleblower!

A bio-lab inspector? The way he was dressed in those photos?

Okay. So what if Dad knew he was a fake, and planned a sting? Dad could have given Hasan stuff to set him up, but it wasn't viruses or spores, it was innocent stuff like flour and foot powders—only before Dad could spring his trap, the cops jumped.

How old are you, Sami? Two?

Fine, I don't have the answers. All I know is, sure Dad's strict, and he makes me mad, and he's embarrassed me more times than I can remember. But he's not this evil, wild-eyed maniac.

What does evil look like, Sami? If monsters looked like monsters, we'd know who to run from. But they don't. The scariest monsters look like family and friends. They're the ones that get you. The ones you trust. You let them into your heart, and then it's too late. They've got you. You're dead. Ask Andy. He thought he knew his dad too.

No! I hit my head over and over, but the voice gets louder. I grab the photo of me and Dad, smash the frame face down on the floor, and shove it, hard, under my bed. I imagine the splintered glass tearing into the paper, shredding Dad's face.

The ceiling and the floor are spinning.

I run to the washroom and throw up.

Twenty-six

Next morning I enter the Academy from the side door to hang out in my cubbyhole. But when I arrive, there's a sign taped under the stairs: SABIRI'S SPIDER HOLE. It's from Eddy. It's got to be. How does he know I come here? Who found out? Who told him?

One thing's for sure: I've lost my safe place. If I'm trapped here now, I'm dead.

But there's a bright spot. Wednesdays and Thursdays the schedule flips, and today's a Wednesday; I get History first period. I figure I'll be safe in Mr. Bernstein's room. But when I get there, I find the door is locked.

I decide to hide out in the can just down the hall. It's empty. I enter a stall, lock the door, and sit cross-legged on the toilet lid so no one'll know I'm here.

Two minutes of silence, except for the drip in the far sink. Then Eddy's gang barges in from the hall. They're laughing, goofing off. Sounds of pissing at the urinals. The paper towel dispenser working overtime.

Then all of a sudden, the can goes quiet.

Eddy whistles softly. "Sa-biiiii-ri . . . ? Where arrrrre you? Sa-biiiii-ri . . . ?"

Oh god, they know I'm here. They've known all along.

Eddy knocks on my stall. "Can Sammy come out and play?"

I stay very still.

"I asked you a question, sand monkey."

My heart flips. "I'm taking a dump. Do you mind?"

"With your feet up?" he mocks.

Group laughter. One of the laughs is coming from overhead. I look up. It's Mark Greeley. He's standing on the toilet lid in the stall to my right, staring down at me over the partition. "Hi there, terror boy."

"Screw off!"

"No way, terror boy!" It's Eddy, hanging over the partition to my left. He grabs my ear, pulls hard. My feet go to the floor. One of his crew grabs my ankles from

203

under the stall door and yanks. I fall backward and crack my head on the bowl as he tries to haul me out. I cling to the base of the toilet, but I'm half outside the stall. The other goons kick me in the gut. I let go. They're all over me.

"Waterboard the little shit!" Eddy shouts.

Suddenly, my legs are in the air, my arms pinned. I'm lowered headfirst into a dirty toilet. I try to twist away, but Eddy grabs me by the hair and forces my face under the water.

"Your dad's a traitor," he shouts. "Say it!" He pulls my head up.

"No!" I cough.

He shoves me back under. I can't think, can't breathe. He hauls my head up. "He's a fucking terrorist! Say it! Say it!"

"You're the terrorist!" I choke.

Eddy smashes my head back into the bowl. I'm gonna pass out, drown, die—or even worse, say anything they want—when out of nowhere Mr. Bernstein yells, "What's going on?" And they drop me hard against the porcelain and run, and I'm on my knees sobbing, and I can't stop, I can't, and Mr. Bernstein kneels beside me, and he hugs me and says, "It's okay, it's over, they've gone."

Only they're back.

"Perverts!" Eddy shouts, as he shoots a cell-phone video of Bernstein holding me.

Mr. Bernstein throws up a hand. "Get out of here!"

But Eddy's already in the corridor. "Perverts in the can! You gotta see this! We got perverts in the can!"

Mr. Bernstein cleans me up and brings me to the office as first period starts. Our class is unsupervised, but he says this is more important. He reports the fight to the secretary and asks to speak to Mr. McGregor.

"Mr. McGregor's in a meeting with Mr. Samuels," Ms. James says. "I'll have him call you down the minute he's through."

We head to History. Halfway down the hall, we hear a roar from Mr. Bernstein's classroom. Teachers stick their heads into the corridor. I grit my teeth as we walk through the door.

The whole class is crowded around Eddy. He's showing the video.

They all freeze when they see us.

"Take your seats," Mr. Bernstein barks. They do. He gives Eddy a dead cold look. "To the office. Now."

Eddy winks at the class and slouches out the door,

holding up his cell. Within seconds, disturbances flicker up and down the hall. My stomach heaves. He's forwarded the video. I'll bet the whole school's seeing it. For all I know, he's put it on YouTube.

Mr. Bernstein tries to carry on, but ten minutes later there's a knock on the door. A teacher on a spare. "Mr. Samuels and Mr. McGregor would like to see you and Sabiri," he says. "I'm here to hold the fort."

Mr. Bernstein and I arrive at the office as Eddy's leaving.

"Get back in there," Mr. Bernstein orders.

"Mr. Samuels let me go, *sir*," Eddy smirks and saunters down the hall.

Mr. Bernstein goes red, but he hasn't got time to waste on Eddy. "Wait there," he says to me, pointing at the bench by the sign-in, and he storms past Ms. James, into Mr. Samuels' office. "What's Eddy Harrison doing in the halls?" he demands. "I sent him here to be dealt with."

"This meeting isn't about Eddy Harrison," Mr. Samuels says. "You may wish to close the door."

"No. Whatever you have to say to me, you say it out loud."

"As you wish. Mr. McGregor and I have been watching a most disturbing video."

"I was comforting a boy who'd had his head shoved in a toilet!"

"All we know is what we see, and what our clients will see," Mr. McGregor says.

Mr. Samuels chimes in. "This week, the Academy was rocked by an association with terrorism. That video of you is the last thing we need. The Academy is a respected institution. We won't have that respect eroded on our watch. Do yourself a favor, Isaac. Retire on sick leave. We'll buy out the rest of your contract."

"You're joking," Mr. Bernstein exclaims. "Over this?"

"No," Mr. Samuels says. "Consider this the last straw. We have complaints about your teaching methods on file going back years. Including three e-mails just yesterday, from angry parents whose sons report that you compared them to Nazis."

"I didn't."

"Care to go through a public investigation? There's also the issue of discipline: The other day, we understand, there were fireworks in your classroom. This morning, a near-riot. You've had a long and happy career at the Academy, Isaac. We'd hate to see it end in disgrace. The choice is yours."

A long pause.

"What's going to happen to Sabiri?" Mr. Bernstein asks.

"Sabiri has vandalized school property, sworn in class, and been implicated in a fight on Roosevelt Trail," Mr. McGregor says. "We've done everything to redeem him. Detentions. A suspension. Nothing's worked. We're left with expulsion."

"You two are quite a piece of work."

Mr. Samuels ignores him. "Your second period class will be canceled. You may take that time to collect your personal effects."

Mr. Bernstein leaves the principal's office, shoulders back, jaw firm.

"Sabiri, you're up," Mr. Samuels says.

"I already heard," I say, and follow Mr. Bernstein out the door.

He walks me to my locker. It's like he's somewhere else. "When I came here, the field house didn't exist. The football scores were painted on plywood squares that slid along metal grooves."

I hesitate. "What are you going to do about your job?"

He leans his back against the wall. "In my glory days, I'd fight. Today, who knows? By the time the fight'd be over, I'd be older than death. Maybe I should see this as an opportunity. Howard loves to travel. And it'd be nice to spend time with our grandkids."

Howard? Grandkids? I want to ask, but I don't.

Mr. Bernstein blinks. "Enough about me. You being expelled. This, we fight."

"Sir, no." I open my locker and cram my stuff into my gym bag and knapsack. "Now I'll get to be with my buddies at Meadowvale Secondary." That is, if the school will take me. And if Andy and Marty are still my buddies. And if Dad isn't locked up forever, and Mom doesn't drop dead, and I don't end up in a group home.

I'm good at faking Happy, but Bernstein's a mind reader. He tilts his head. "What's the matter? Apart from everything."

I slump against my locker door. "I'm scared."

"Me too, sometimes. But here's what I tell myself." He puts his hand on my shoulder. "We can't choose what life throws at us. But we can choose what we do about it. Our choices are who we are. And who we are—that, no one can take away from us."

"Like that's a big help."

"Right," he smiles. "Big advice from a man who just got 'retired.'"

I smile back. We stand there, not knowing what to say or do. "Well, then." I get my knapsack on my back and hoist my gym bag. "Guess I should go."

He nods. "Since you're no longer my student," he says, "let me just say: If you ever need help, or someone to listen, I'm in the phone book under Howard Taylor, on Beachwood."

"Thank you. Thanks."

And all of a sudden I get this brain glitch: Phone book. Numbers. Names. Addresses. Why didn't I think of this before?

"Mr. Bernstein, I'm really sorry, but I gotta go. Now."

And before I can blink, I'm in the library at a computer. I google "Toronto" + "telephone directory" and choose the first site on the page. Then I click + "Find a Person."

In the Name field, I type: Hasan, T.

Up come eight Hasan, Ts, with phone numbers and addresses.

I whip out my wallet and find the paper with the Toronto numbers I copied from Dad's computer. I check the one that I thought belonged to a girlfriend. Bingo. It belongs to T. Hasan on Gerrard Street.

I write down the address, log off, tear out of the

building, and race down Roosevelt Trail, gulping air as fast as I can.

I don't know everything, but I know this: Dad wasn't calling a woman. He was calling Tariq Hasan. The voice on the answering machine must've been Hasan's wife, mom, girlfriend, sister, who knows.

The good news: Dad wasn't having an affair. The bad news: He knew Hasan *before* he went to Toronto and ended up in that FBI photo—which makes the e-mail in court look even worse.

How did Dad get connected to a terrorist? What did they talk about? What did Dad pack up for him from "storage"? Where's the package now? What were "the plans" Dad said he admired?

Only Dad knows. And Hasan. Hasan's the key. Without him, Dad's finished for sure. But Hasan's in hiding. He could be anywhere.

No. Wait. I know how to catch him. And I'm the only one who can.

Andy and Marty.

I need them.

Now!

PART FOUR

PART FOUR

Twenty-seven

I hit Meadowvale Secondary at lunch break. It's a zoo. Crowds of students lounge around the front steps, stuff their faces on the lawn, and catch a few autumn rays on the bleachers by the track to the right. The smokers cluster on the sidewalk across the street, off school property. I recognize a few of them from my eighth-grade class; if they see me, they don't show it.

Andy and Marty. Where are they? A stream of cars shuttles out of the student parking lot. Damn, I'll bet they've gone to the mall for a burger.

But I'm wrong.

"Sammy!"

I look to my left. Andy's loping toward me. Marty's

right behind him, wiping chocolate off his face. "Buddy, what's up? You okay?"

They hustle me to the Deathmobile. We drive out of the lot, onto the main road, and shoot past the mall and the box stores. The whole time they're blabbing away, and I've never felt so good in my life.

"Why didn't you call?" I demand.

"Why didn't *you*?" they toss back.

It turns out their folks took their cells; they were freaked that Homeland Security might tap all their phones since I was a friend of their kids. Andy's mom was a little drunk: "If we've been bugged," she said, "I hope the FBI heard your goddamn father moaning for his goddamn whores!" But Andy and Marty didn't give up. They tried me a bunch of times from pay phones. Those must have been the calls I thought were from cranks and deleted.

"We wanted to knock on your door," Andy says, "but there were all those cameras. Plus with everything else going down, we figured you didn't need us bugging you."

"Are you kidding? I wanted to see you so bad. I thought you'd bailed."

"Bailed?" Marty exclaims. "Insult us or what!"

"I told Marty you'd find us when you needed us,"

Andy says. "The last two days, we've been waiting out front, before and after school and at lunch."

"I've been going through Mall Withdrawal," Marty moans.

I grin. "So everything's good!"

"Great. It's so fantastic to see you again!"

I tell them about getting expelled, and how I'll probably end up back with them. They whoop so loud I practically go deaf, and I have to scream at Andy to watch out or he'll slam into the van in front of us.

We turn into Fenton Park. Andy pulls under the shade of a maple at the end of the tennis courts. A couple of old guys are batting a ball. Apart from them, we're alone. We get out of the car, stretch, and check the nearby picnic tables for a Bird-Shit-Free Zone. Andy and Marty claim a clean patch of table top. I stand.

"Guess you've heard about Dad's e-mail to the Brotherhood of Martyrs," I say. Talk about a conversation stopper.

Andy hesitates. "So what happens now?"

"Not much. Except . . ." I glance over at a squirrel, try to make it look like what I'm about to say is no big deal. "Except you have to get me into Canada."

Andy shakes his head like he heard wrong. "Say what?"

"The thing is, I have to get into Canada, and I don't have a driver's license, much less a car. Even if I did, I'd get stopped at the border, what with my name and Dad being my Dad and all. So I need to cross where they don't check, which means by water, which means I need you to take me on the Catalina. Cuz I don't have a boat, and even if I did, how would I steer it? I'd plow into an island or something."

Marty scrunches his nose. "Are you on drugs?"

"No."

"Well you should be. Heavy-duty prescription."

Andy fishes in his pocket. "Want some Ritalin?"

"Guys, I'm serious. I need to get into Canada. Tomorrow, if possible."

"It's the middle of a school week."

"Since when have you had a problem cutting class? Tell your folks, I don't know, *The National Enquirer*'s chasing you for a story. Or a pervert saw you on the news and is stalking you. Whatever. The point is, convince them you need to get away, or you'll say or do something that'll get the whole family in trouble."

"Whoa!" Andy interrupts. "Why do you need to get into Canada?"

"I have things to do in Toronto. You can take me in

that Chevy you've got mothballed at the cottage. It's just a few hours' drive. You and Marty can see the Jays, the Leafs, go up the CN Tower, take your pick. I'll do my stuff, we'll meet up and come home. Over and done in a day, two tops. It'll be fun. What do you say?"

"I say this isn't funny," Andy says. "What 'stuff' do you have to do in Toronto? Why is it so important it can't wait?"

"Don't ask questions, you won't get in trouble."

"Don't answer questions, you won't get anywhere," he shoots back.

I bang my fists on the table. "I thought you were my friends."

"We are," Andy says. "But you gotta trust us. What's the deal?"

"It's about Dad." I try to keep my voice steady. "He says he's innocent. I know it looks bad, but what if he is? I have to help him."

"How?"

"By getting the truth. And that means finding Tariq Hasan."

"The terrorist?" Marty asks, like maybe I mean some other Tariq, like Tariq the plumber or something.

"Yeah, the terrorist."

Now they look at me like I've *really* lost it.

"And how exactly do you plan to do that?" Andy asks, his eyebrows rising off his forehead.

"First, I have to get to Toronto. That's why I need you guys. I found Hasan's phone number. I even tried it. I have his address too."

"So what?" Andy says. "Hasan's split."

"Yeah," Marty echoes. "You think he's holed up in his closet or something? Maybe hiding behind his shower curtain? You think he's, like, 'Hey the FBI's on my tail, not to worry, I'll just paint myself the color of the wall, blend in, yeah that'll do it.'"

"Face it, you won't find Hasan," Andy says. "Nobody knows where he is. Not the FBI. Not Homeland Security. Nobody."

"That's not true," I fire back. "Somebody always knows something. Look at gang crimes. Almost every time there's a shooting, there's witnesses. But nobody snitches. Why? Loyalty? Fear? Lots of reasons. Well, this is like that. Wherever Hasan is, there's got to be somebody feeding him, protecting him. Maybe a girlfriend or a relative. There was a woman on his voice mail—maybe her, or a friend of hers, or a friend of his, or a neighbor, or someone from his mosque."

"Okay," Andy says, "but whoever it is isn't talking. So why would they talk to you?"

"Because," I tap his chest, "I'm the son of Hasan's supposed accomplice—the son of category-four bio-lab director Dr. Arman Sabiri, aka Dr. Death."

I let that sink in, then press ahead. "According to the e-mail they read in court, Dad had stuff packed and ready for Hasan. The arrests happened before Hasan could leave Toronto to get it. So if I'm Hasan, I want that package. And when my contact brings me word that Dr. Death's son has dropped by my old apartment, I'm gonna wonder if maybe he's got it."

Andy and Marty stare at me. Only this time, not like I'm crazy.

"It's true, I don't know who's hiding Hasan," I say. "And it's true I can't hunt him down. But I don't need to. All I have to do is show up. Then Hasan will find *me*."

Andy goes slack-jawed. "You're going to turn yourself into bait."

I nod. "People don't talk to cops. But I'm not a cop. I'm a short, skinny brown kid. I can slip in under the radar."

"Hold up, this isn't a video game," Marty exclaims. "No offense, Sammy, but you're hardly a hero. You can't even stand up to that Eddy guy at the Academy."

"Who cares about Eddy? This is my dad we're talking about. You get that, right?"

"What I get is this is way past borderline crazy. It's right off the friggin' map. No way the three of us can do this. You need the FBI, somebody serious, to go with you."

"No!" I circle the table. "If Hasan suspects he's being set up, my plan's dead. Besides, do you think the FBI would let me get close? The second they'd know where Hasan is, they'd move in. He'd be killed in a shootout, or locked up, with everything he knows classified forever. Either way, Dad's screwed."

"He's kind of screwed already," Andy says.

"Andy's right," Marty piles on. "You're risking a lot for nothing. You're asking us to risk a lot too."

"I'm not! Hasan has no reason to hurt me; I'm the son of his 'buddy,' after all. As for you guys, there's no way he'll ever know you exist. The worst that can happen to you is the school will mark you absent." I lean against the table. "Anyway, I need an answer: Are you with me?"

Andy's foot taps like Thumper. Marty wriggles. They glance at each other, then down at the grass.

I exhale. "So that's how it is?"

Andy shrugs helplessly. "It's too much. It's too fast. Maybe if you asked some other time . . ."

"There is no other time." I check my watch. "You two better get back to school. Wouldn't want you late for class."

I turn on my heel and march to the Deathmobile. Andy and Marty follow. Andy starts the engine, turns on some music. We head out of the lot. Nobody says anything. Andy keeps his eyes on the road. Marty and me look off at whatever. We drive past the box stores.

"Want me to drop you at home?" Andy asks quietly.

I shake my head. "Leave me at the side of the highway."

"What?"

"I asked for your help. You said no. Fine. I'll make other arrangements."

"You're going to Toronto on your own?" Marty blinks. "How?"

"None of your business."

"Of course it's our business," Andy says. "You're our friend."

"It sure doesn't feel like it."

"Sammy—"

"Look, stop the car. Let me off."

"No way," Andy speeds up. "Not if you're gonna do something crazy. We need to talk."

"What for? I've got stuff to do and I'm doing it. You can't stop me."

"Who said anything about stopping you? It's just—" Andy grips the wheel. "What you want—it's enormous."

"Who cares? If Dad's innocent and I do nothing—how do I live with that?"

"And if he's guilty?" Marty blurts.

"At least I'll know the truth."

Andy turns off the music. The silence is unbearable. We drive, none of us knowing what to say or do. Finally Andy blurts out, "You talk about living with something? If you go alone and get hurt, how are Marty and I supposed to live with *that*?"

"That's for you to figure out."

Marty wipes his hands on his jeans.

Andy drums his fingers on the steering wheel. "What you said in the park makes sense," he says at last. "Hasan has no reason to hurt you. And he doesn't know who we are. Hey, you may not even get to see him anyway. So maybe there's no risk at all. Maybe. Maybe, maybe, maybe."

Andy pulls over to the side of the road. He rests his head on the steering wheel, then throws it back against the head rest. "Okay. Give us the night to work on our folks," he says quietly. "I'll offer Mom to close up the cottage for the winter. I'll tell her it'll take a day or two, and I'll need Marty's help. I'll say it's the perfect time cuz nothing's happening at school what with everyone talking about you-know-what. Once Mom's on board, she'll call Marty's mom and we should be good."

"You fine with that?" I ask Marty.

He glances out the window. "You calling me a coward?"

It's not exactly an answer, but I let it pass.

"One thing." Andy looks me straight in the eye. "If we go with you, you let us know wherever you're going. If there's a problem, we need to be close by to get help."

"Okay."

"Another thing," he adds. "If you see Hasan, the second you leave his hideout, we call the cops."

"Absolutely."

"Absolutely, absolutely," Marty says. His cheeks are a mass of red blotches.

Andy gives Marty a buddy-punch to the shoulder. "Who knows, Marty? If we find Hasan, maybe there'll be a reward. You can get a lifetime supply of Ben & Jerry's. Just remember to bring a clean pair of underwear in case you have an accident."

Now all of Marty's face goes red. "Ha ha. So what time do we meet?"

"I'll pick you up at five thirty," Andy tells him.

"A.M.?"

"Whaddaya think, the middle of the afternoon? Of course A.M. It's called the 'Element of Surprise.' We don't want to be followed, so no pissing around. I hit your driveway, you're in the front seat, good to go."

We synchronize our watches.

Andy turns to me. "Sammy, in case anyone's watching your house, don't use the front door. When you hear my car, slip through your backyard hedge and run across the golf course. We'll be over the fence from the twelfth hole, by the little park on Braddock Crescent, five thirty-five. Got it?"

"Got it."

Twenty-eight

When I get home, there's a note on the kitchen table: "I'm upstairs with a migraine. Please do not disturb. Stuffed peppers in the fridge. Love, Mom."

The phone light's flashing. Two messages. The first is from Mr. McGregor: "I'm sorry to inform you, blah, blah, blah, school fees cannot be refunded." I press DELETE.

The second is from the pharmacy: "Neda, Deb here. Don't take it bad. You know how people are. I'm sure Frank'll get your shift back once things have settled down. Call me if you need me."

Frank'll get your shift back? I play the message again. I heard right. Mom's lost her job.

I throw open the fridge door, really mad, but before

I can get anything, I go dizzy. I sink into a chair at the kitchen table and drop my head between my knees. Mom's unemployed, Dad's in jail. Where's our money going to come from? How'll we pay for Dad's lawyer? Will we have to sell the house? Will we end up on the street?

I press my hands against the back of my head. "It's going to be all right. It's going to be all right." Oh yeah?

I forget about supper and go to bed. I have to be rested for tomorrow. I have to clear Dad's name. Not just for him, but for Mom and me. Our lives depend on it.

Sometime after midnight, I eventually drift off. I wake up at four, drenched in sweat. For the first time since I can remember, I have this need to pray. I wash my hands, face, and feet in the laundry tub. Lay a blanket on my bedroom floor as a prayer rug. Face Mecca, and begin to bow, kneel, prostrate myself, praying in Arabic for God's blessing.

I've prayed the first chapter of the Qur'an so many times, I've stopped hearing the words. But now, in the predawn dark, they ring clear. Each syllable connects me to a power bigger than myself, a world of others praying the same words. My forehead tingles. I'm not alone. I'm not afraid. I'm going to save Dad, my family, Inshallah.

* * *

Five thirty. Dead quiet. I've packed a change of underwear, shirt, socks, and a toothbrush in my knapsack. I leave a note for Mom by the coffee maker:

"Hope your migraine's better. I'm with Andy and Marty. Couldn't ask for permission cuz you were asleep. If I'm not back tonight, don't worry, I'll call. Everything's fine. Love, Sami." I feel a bit guilty about the permission bit. I mean, it's true, but I wouldn't have asked for permission even if she'd been awake.

I hear Andy's car.

I grab my knapsack and split through the backyard. A wriggle and I'm through the hedge, onto the golf course. There's no moon. In my black jeans and hoodie, I'm next to invisible. Even so, I crouch low and skitter like a ferret to the shadows by the rough. I zigzag across fairways, through sand traps, around water obstacles. Head for the elms on the twelfth fairway. Scramble over the fence. Race to the street.

No Andy.

A heartbeat, and the Deathmobile swings onto the crescent. I dive into the back before it stops, and lie flat till we're out of the subdivision.

Andy's pumped, like he's mainlined a quart of espresso. Before we split up yesterday, I gave him Hasan's address.

He got directions from the cottage to Hasan's doorstep, courtesy of Google. He also downloaded a ton of stuff: points of interest along the way, Toronto maps and transit routes, things to see if the mission's a bust, and a list of youth hostels in case we stay over. It's all stuffed in a file folder code-named *Geography: Independent Study Unit: Toronto Field Trip.*

"On top, I've put a map of the downtown for each of you," he says. "Note the red star at the corner of Yonge and Dundas Streets. There's an open-air plaza there, opposite this big mall, the Eaton Centre. It'll be our rendezvous point if we get separated. Put your copy in a pocket now, before you forget."

We do as we're told. Mine goes next to the ballpoint pen in the front pocket of my jeans.

"If you spent as much time researching essays, you'd get straight As," I say.

"Yeah, well, that's not all I've got us," Andy winks, his voice a tickle of mystery. As we turn onto the State Thruway, he reaches across Marty and pulls a heavy-duty paper bag out of the glove compartment. "Check my little surprise."

"What is it?"

"Protection," he grins. "There's one for each of us."

"No way, Andy!" I freak. "No guns."

"Don't wet your pants. Cell phones."

"But our folks returned our cells in case of problems at the cottage," Marty says.

"Yeah, with instructions not to call Sammy. And don't think they won't check." Andy drives with his left hand while reaching into the bag with his right. He tosses us each a piece of plastic crap. "These are burn phones from Dollar Value. They come with a little time. No subscriber ID. You use 'em and ditch 'em. Untraceable. Exactly what we need to keep in touch, in case Sammy gets in trouble."

Way to make me feel good. Not.

What with it being midweek, fall, the Alexandria Bay marina's pretty dead. Just a few retirees in jackets and wool caps, hunched over their fishing poles at the end of the pier.

"Think normal," Andy whispers.

We buy bait from a vending machine, to make it look like we're out to catch fish instead of terrorists. Then we make our way to Pier 4, Well 22.

"There she is," Andy says. "Good old *Cirrhosis of the River.*"

We stash our stuff, get the life jackets out of the storage bins, loosen the moorings, and cast off. The old man that Andy always waves at is here again, stomping his feet in the sharp morning air. He gives us a nod, blows into his hands. A squint at the sun, and we're skipping into open water.

I feel queasy. Not sure if it's fear or the drive-thru McBreakfast. I call to Andy to slow down. He makes like he can't hear me over the bay breeze. I cling to the side of the Catalina and pretend it's tomorrow, today's already happened, and we're safe.

I'm better by the time we dock at the cottage. Marty commandeers the can for his morning extravaganza. Minutes later he runs out, screaming, "Bats! Bats!" Turns out he disturbed a baby bat hanging off the curtain rod. And this idiot's going to help me track down a terrorist ringleader? What am I thinking?

Andy goes to the kitchen. When they're away, the Js disconnect the Chevy's battery and store it in a cookie box over the fridge. It keeps the battery charged and the car from being a thief magnet. By nine thirty, Andy's got it hooked up. The tires are a little soft, but good enough to get to the gas station up the road.

He opens the trunk and takes a wrench and a tire

iron out of a plastic crate. He whaps each of them against his hand. I hope he's not planning to play hero. All the same, he's the only one of us who can take care of things in a jam.

Andy's pants are a maze of zippers and Velcro; they're the Swiss army knife of khakis. He slips the wrench down a side pocket along his calf, and slides the tire iron under the driver's seat. I pretend not to notice.

We lock up the cottage and double-check the dock to make sure the Catalina's secure. I take a last look at the waterfront. Will I ever see it again?

"Sammy, get your ass in gear," Andy hollers.

And we're off.

Twenty-nine

We're on the 401 to Toronto, a multilane highway packed with trucks. It's fast but hardly the scenic route. I check my watch every few minutes. Calm myself with prayers.

"Pickering," Andy says. "We're getting close. Check out the nuclear power plant to the left." I stare at a wasteland of concrete visible from the highway and the lake beyond. From the air, an easy bull's-eye. "You can read about it in my folder. Wild stuff," he says.

The wild stuff is a news story Mr. Bhanjee had stressed in one of his pep talks: Shortly after 9/11, Canada's national police, the RCMP, arrested twenty-three Pakistanis and a South Indian on terror charges. A bunch of them were on expired student visas, attending this sketchy madrassa. But the reason they got arrested was they were learning to pilot planes over the nuclear plant. The raid was called Project Thread, but the case unraveled. It turns out every flying school in the area had the same flight plan. And why were their flight plans over a nuclear power plant? Because of the nice view!

"Officials had to admit they had no evidence," Mr. Bhanjee said. "The young men were released without ever going to trial. Moral of the story: Officials make mistakes. Innocent people can go free."

Right, but after how much time in jail for nothing? And then what? According to the news item, they got deported to Pakistan, where they've been hassled by police forever after, treated like criminals, unable to get a job. This is a happy ending?

Anyway, what's it have to do with Dad? None of those guys had e-mail, cell, and video evidence against them. And just because authorities mess up, doesn't mean they mess up all the time. Innocent people get arrested, sure, but not everyone who's arrested is innocent. No, stop it, I can't think this way.

"Toronto," Andy shouts. "We're here. Watch for the Don Valley Parkway."

In no time, we're zipping toward the city center, along a highway that snakes through woods, parks, ridges, and ravines. To our right, off in the distance, the CN Tower rises over the skyline. According to Google, Hasan lives a few minutes from here, in an area called the India Bazaar.

We swerve between cars onto a tight exit ramp. A sharp loop and we merge with traffic mounting a steep, winding hill. At the top, Andy glances at the map and pulls a dogleg onto Greenwood Avenue. Soon, we're at a main intersection: Danforth.

A few hundred yards off, I spot women wearing hijabs and some men in Islamic dress, milling outside a nondescript building. A mosque, I'll bet. Noon prayers.

"Any second," Andy says. He grips the steering wheel. We go down a hill, a massive transit shed to our right, fenced-off town homes to our left. We go under an overpass and along a block of rundown houses pasted to the sidewalk.

Suddenly—Gerrard Street. Hasan. On one corner, a pizza joint. Opposite, a mini-mart with a small parking lot.

"Pull in," I say. "Let's call Hasan's, see if anybody's home."

"Good idea, if they'll answer," Andy says. "But don't waste your cell. Use the pay phone, side of the building. We'll be across the street getting takeout."

"No ham or sausage," I say.

"Hunh?"

"It's haraam."

"Haraam?" Andy looks at me weird. "Like the food list your dad used to send to the cottage?"

"You got a problem with that?"

"No," Andy says, hands in the air. "I just never thought you were religious is all."

"I don't know what I am. I just don't want to take chances."

I get out of the car and make the call. It goes through. The line's in service, but I get the voice message. "Blah, blah, blah, you know what to do." Beep.

This time, I *do* know what to do. I call again and again and again and again. If anybody's home, I'm gonna bug them till they pick up screaming. At last, just as I start to think everyone really *is* out, I get an actual person. Her.

"Who is it?"

I freeze.

"Whoever you are, I've had it with the goddamn harassment," she steams. "The line's bugged, so watch your sorry ass or I'll get Officer Dipshit, who's listening in, to charge you. By the way, Officer, have a nice wank." Click. I smile. She sounds like me.

Andy honks the horn, and I hop back into the car. We all grab slices of pizza as Andy pulls onto Gerrard. The pizza tastes as cardboard as the box: dried-out dough with a smear of tomato sauce and a handful of mushroom bits that look like fried roaches. We wolf it down anyway. Andy tries to avoid the street-car tracks while Marty and I look out the windows, searching for numbers.

The India Bazaar. At first, I don't get the name. I mean, we're driving along your basic two-story, flat-roofed McStrip. There's rooming houses, a gas station, doughnut shop, coin laundry, greasy spoons, and a pair of grubby bars. Above the stores, some sad apartments, the windows covered by dusty drapes, torn roller blinds, and tin foil, the odd glass pane replaced by plywood.

Then, out of nowhere, we're in the middle of it: a nonstop wall of Indian and Pakistani restaurants, halal grocery stores, an Islamic book center, and jewelry and fabric shops with windows full of silks and saris. Some of the merchandise spills onto the street: racks of brilliant scarves next to sweet trays, and produce stands with crates of mangoes, lichees on the twig, and ripe pomegranates stacked amid a jostle of copper pots and pans, and two-foot stainless steel shish kebab skewers.

I squint hard. "Hasan's place should be right around here."

"Know what's weird?" Marty says. "Hasan is on the loose, and people are out doing their thing."

"Why not?" Andy says. "He's hardly hiding in the area. Besides, we've still got that unidentified terrorist around Meadowvale, and people are at the mall and stuff."

I spot the narrow blue door from the news. "That's the door. The number."

We go to the next corner. There's a small library across the street to the north. It's strangely familiar. The set of cement steps, the shaded window. Where have I seen it? My god. The FBI photos. It's where Dad met Hasan.

We turn south onto a side street. There's a lane that separates the back of the Gerrard Street stores from a mess of low-fenced residential yards that stretches down to the next big intersection. No wonder Hasan escaped so easily. All the stores on his strip are connected, each with a back fire escape and a row of second-floor apartment windows. Even with cops breaking in at the front and back, if he was on the flat roof, he could dash the length of the block, drop anywhere, pop into a backyard, and disappear in a flash.

We park.

"Okay, Sammy," Andy says. "Marty and I'll be inside the library, watching you go to Hasan's. If the woman doesn't answer the buzzer, knock till your knuckles bleed."

"Not so fast," I say. "We don't want attention. Even without camera crews, there'll likely be surveillance from a car or a window across the street. Maybe at the back too, from one of the houses across the lane. I'll start with a casual stroll-by. Meet you in five."

They head to the library. I put my hoodie up, and do a slow walk along the street, checking out the produce stalls, the silk racks. The door leading up to Hasan's apartment is squeezed between two restaurants.

I pretend to read the vegetarian menu in the window to the right, but my eyes are on his door frame. There's six buzzers. The stairs beyond the door must lead up to a hallway of apartments running across several first-floor businesses. Each of the buzzers has a name beside it—except for buzzer four, where the name's been scratched out. No surprise whose apartment it is or why the name's been removed.

I turn away from the menu and saunter down the

street, then cross over and double back to the library. The guys are at a table in the teen section. Marty's got a graphic novel. Andy's drumming his knees. I fill them in.

"So what do we do now?" Marty asks. For the first time ever, he's looking at *me* when he says it. Andy's glancing my way too. It's a little overwhelming. Especially since I realize we've been incredibly stupid.

"Here's the thing," I say. "Hasan's friend or relative is in Apartment Four. But the place is probably bugged. So problem one is, if I tell her what I'd planned—that I'm Sabiri's son and I've got something for Tariq—I'll be in deep shit. Whoever's doing surveillance will think I'm a terrorist too. Right?"

Andy frowns. "And problem two?"

"Problem two: Even if I just press her buzzer, the wiretap will pick up the buzz. Whoever's watching the place will know I want to see her. Bingo, they'll be snapping my picture like crazy. And for what? I mean, the way she was on the phone, she won't let me in unless I spill who I am. Which, of course, I can't—because of problem one."

"So we should sit outside on the steps, watch the door for when she comes out, and tail her," Andy says.

I shake my head. "That's problems three and four.

Three: She's likely being tailed already. If we start following her, we'll be followed too. Four: There are six apartments up there, and we don't know what she looks like. A woman comes out of the building, how do we know it's her? Who would we follow? Even if we could, which we can't."

An awful silence. A fly lands on the table, cleans its wings. Marty's stomach grumbles.

"Want to go back to the car?" he says. "Finish the rest of the pizza?"

"How can you think about eating?" Andy snaps.

"Sorry, I just thought—"

I smack my head. "The pizza! Marty, you're a genius!"

"Me? Hunh!"

I hunker over the table. "I have a plan."

Thirty

One thing at a time.

I write a note to Hasan's girlfriend and put it in my pocket. I switch hoodies with Marty; it's a little baggy, but it makes me look different in case anyone took my picture before. I leave the guys, go to the car, and get our pizza box.

I'm ready.

No, I'm not. I mean, what am I doing? I'm walking to a terrorist's door with a pizza box! It's like I'm in a dream. My feet are moving on their own; I can't stop them. So many times, things look easy, then turn into something else—like that trip to Hermit Island. Or go out of control—like with Mr. Bernstein in the can. Or like now. Am I going to die? Why can't we know the end of things at the beginning?

I'm at the blue door.

Hasan's place is Apartment Four, but I can't let anyone guess that's where I'm going. I press buzzer five and hope whoever's there will let me in. I wait.

I want to run, but I'm caught in this wave; it's dragging me out, I can't stop it.

I press the buzzer again.

Breathe. I'm not doing anything wrong. I'm just delivering a pizza. If I clear Dad, that's good, right? Or if I find Hasan, I can report it—which is also good, right? And Andy and Marty are across the street with cells in case anything goes wrong. I'm fine. I'm safe. There's no problem.

So if there's no problem, why are my feet sweating? Shut up. Don't be a coward.

One last try at Apartment Five. No answer.

I try buzzer one. Nothing.

Buzzer two. Somebody's gotta be home besides Hasan's friend.

Buzz. Buzz. Buzzzzzzzzzzzzz.

Somebody, anybody, let me in. I've been standing here too long. It's gotta look weird. Why? It's a pizza delivery. Whoever's watching could think the person I'm buzzing is holed up in the can or getting their money.

What's strange about that? Nothing—except the pizza box is empty. So? Who's gonna know that?

Apartment Two answers. There's a bunch of static over the intercom, a TV in the background: "Who is it?"

"Pizza delivery."

Crackle—"I didn't order pizza"—crackle.

"It's for Apartment Five."

Crackle—"So buzz Apartment Five." The intercom goes dead.

I try Apartment Two again. Hold it down forever.

Crackle—"I said, try—"

"Their buzzer doesn't work!"

Pause. A click on the door lock. Apartment Two lets me in.

The stairwell is a dirty mustard color. It smells of fried fish. If Mom was here, she'd be reaching for her hand sanitizer. I make sure not to touch the railing.

Apartment Two is watching a really loud show. They don't bother to check me out. I go down the hall to Hasan's place and take the note out of my pocket. It reads:

SABIRI JUNIOR IS LOOKING FOR YOUR FRIEND.
LIBRARY ACROSS THE STREET, TRAVEL SECTION.
DON'T KEEP ME WAITING.

That last bit was Andy's idea, to make me sound tough. Anyway, there's nothing in it that could get me in trouble. At least I don't think so.

I slide the note back and forth under the door before leaving it. Anyone listening in on a wiretap will think someone's just rubbing their foot back and forth. But whoever's inside should hear the rustle.

Flash panic. What if Apartment Two is suspicious about why I haven't knocked at Apartment Five to deliver the pizza? No sweat. I go to Apartment Five. I know that nobody's there from when I buzzed, so I bang hard. "Pizza!"

I have this whole imaginary speech in my head where I say, How do you do, sir? Thanks for the tip. By the way, your buzzer doesn't work. But before I can get out a word, the door is thrown open. There's a big, sweaty guy holding a towel around his waist. Boy is he mad. In the background I see a woman in a bathrobe.

"You the asshole who buzzed?" sweaty guy yells.

"Uh, no."

I race down the hall, ditch the pizza box in the stairwell, and exit onto the street. Sweaty guy wouldn't chase me down the street in a towel, would he? I dodge up the next side street and circle back to the library.

"What happened?" Andy says.

"Don't ask."

"When you ran out of the building, I saw a curtain move," Marty volunteers. "Someone was watching you."

"Hasan's friend, let's hope," I say. "Maybe trying to see what I look like."

I go to the travel section and have the guys take a few books to a table at the end of the aisle. I stand and look over the shelves, like maybe I'm researching a family trip. Hmmm. Where to, Sami? Amsterdam? Australia? France? Germany? I pull out Lonely Planet's *Egypt*.

I'm so busy checking out the pyramids, I almost don't notice the woman standing next to me. She's wearing a gray skirt, black sweater, black nylons, and a niqab. Only her eyes are showing; they're rimmed in liner and mascara. She takes the Fodor's *Mexico*, glances at it, and returns it to the shelf. A piece of paper sticks out slightly over the top.

The woman gets two other books and heads to the checkout counter. I wait till she's gone, then take all five

Mexico books back to the table. With my back to the counter, I pull the paper out of the Fodor's.

It reads:

NORTHEAST CORNER, YONGE AND BLOOR, 5 P.M.

Five o'clock. Two hours from now.

My heart skips. "How do we get there?"

"Easy, dummy," Andy says. "I put maps in the folder, remember?"

"This is real," Marty whispers.

"Yeah, but nothing to worry about." I try to act like I mean it. "Yonge and Bloor, it's a public street corner. There'll be people around. You guys can blend in, be on the lookout for trouble."

"But what if they take you somewhere?" Marty says.

"Follow me, idiot. You've got legs, right?"

Marty starts to rock in his seat. "But what if they stuff you into a car or something?"

"I'll stay in the Chevy," Andy volunteers. "I'll park a few yards from the corner. If they drive you anywhere, I'll follow. I'm good at keeping up in traffic."

"And I have a cell phone, remember," I say. "If I get in over my head, I'll use it." That almost calms me down. Then I flash on me tied up in the trunk of a car, trying to fumble it out of my pocket. Help. Breathe. Breathe.

"Sammy, if we lose you, we'll call for help too," Andy says. "On foot, you won't be far off. Even if you're in a vehicle, we'll have the license number, make, and model, plus we'll be within a few blocks."

"Hold on," I panic. "If I disappear, don't call right away. I could be totally safe, just not able to phone. Like, if I'm talking with Hasan."

Marty's eyes pop. "You're kidnapped and you want us to do nothing?"

"But I might not be kidnapped. They might just have taken me someplace secure. You get the cops involved, things could get ugly. I could become a hostage. If you leave me alone, I could be fine."

"*Could be*," Andy underlines grimly.

Marty blows between his hands. "We should walk," he says. "We should walk, we should walk, we should walk."

No. We're too close. We've come too far. Dad, I won't let you down. Not this time.

I fake a smile. "Take a pill, Marty. Remember, Hasan has no reason to hurt me. That's as true today as it was yesterday." And how true was it yesterday? Hasan's a terrorist. What if he thinks I could give him away?

Andy whittles his ear with a flurry of fingers. "Okay, Sammy. If we lose contact, we'll cross our fingers that you're safe. But you have to promise you'll meet us by nine o'clock at the latest, at the plaza, Yonge and Dundas. It's on the map I gave you. The red star. If you're not there, we go to the cops."

"Fair enough."

Andy grabs our hands. "We gotta think positive, guys. Sammy, we have your back. You'll be fine."

Thirty-one

Yonge and Bloor. Five to five.

No wonder this is the place for the meet. It's city center, rush hour. The cross streets: a snarl of cars, taxis, cyclists, and motorbikes; two lanes in each direction. Shoppers and business types pour through wide glass doors onto crammed sidewalks. They dodge, press, bump each other, or pack in a mass at the traffic lights. Like Andy and Marty, Hasan's people can blend with the crowd easy.

I'm at the northeast corner in front of a skyscraper that stretches the block. Marty's thirty feet away, sitting by a railing up a bank of steps to the building's office complex. It's not a great spot. He's accidentally tripped a few business types working their BlackBerrys while rushing down the stairs, plus taken a briefcase to the head. But it's the only place where he can keep me in sight.

As for Andy? He's circling the block in the Chevy on account of there's no street parking. No standing or stopping either. At a couple of minutes to five—like, *now*—he's supposed to pull over, turn on his flashers, and look under his hood, like his car's dead. We had to cut it tight: If he pulls over too soon, he'll have cops and a tow truck on his ass. But if he's too late, well . . . too late'll be too late, which is what I'm worried about.

I dig my fingernails into my palms. It's no time to be scared.

Major honking down the street. Some kind of jam. And it's five o'clock. Just what I need—Andy, stuck in traffic. Suddenly, relief. Andy's nudging a right turn through a wall of pedestrians at the crosswalk.

"Face the street, Sami."

Did I hear that? I glance over. There's a woman, half turned away: a blonde in her twenties, in a windbreaker, jeans, shades. She laughs into a cell phone, cups her hand over her ear, like she's on a bad connection. "You heard me, Sami," she says in a low voice. "Face the street."

Holy shit. I face the street.

"I have a subway token in my left hand," the woman continues, "At the count of three, I'm going to drop it. You're going to pick it up and follow me. Stay close, but not too close. And never, ever, look at my face. Understood? One, two, three."

I turn as the token hits the pavement. I dive for it, feet everywhere around me. I see it bounce, grab it, leap up. Where is she? I spin around. There. Headed toward a bank of doors. I race after her. This is it. I've crossed the line. There's no way back.

Marty's running down the stairs. Andy's pulling over. But the woman's through the doors. I am too.

We hurry down a few steps, turn right into a tangle of underground shops bursting with crowds, smells, lights, noise. I squeeze my way through. A quick glance back. Andy and Marty are top of the steps, scanning the mob. The woman's ahead of me. She can't see me signal. Let's hope *they* can. I stretch my hand high, wave it like crazy.

We're at a set of glass doors. The subway entrance. We go through. Last check. I see Andy's head bobbing above the crowd. He's catching up.

The doors close behind us. The woman's at a row of turnstiles. She drops her token, gets to the other side. I follow. We turn right, to a set of stairs going down to the tracks.

And now some luck. A wave of arrivals surges up from below. Bottleneck.

It breaks as Andy and Marty burst through the entrance doors. They see me disappearing, race to leap the turnstiles. Andy sails over. Marty splats out. But Andy's bogged down by the arrivals. The man in the token booth bangs his glass.

That's all I see. A new train's pulling in. The woman reaches back, grabs my hand, and pulls me down the last few steps onto the platform.

The train doors open. A heave of bad air; people spill out. We press against the current and force our way in, the last on board.

A whistle blows to clear the doorways. And out of the blue, there's Marty flying down the stairs, arms and legs spinning like pinwheels. He sees me and leaps through the door just down from us. I'm safe.

The doors start to close. A sudden push from the woman. We're back on the platform. I turn to the train. Marty's stuck inside, his face pressed against the glass. "Buddy," he mouths, "I'm sorry." His train hurtles into the tunnel.

"Move it," the woman says.

She's walking faster now. I scramble to keep up, zigzagging through streams of commuters. I bump into a pillar with a map of the subway line. I try to see where I am, but I don't have time; I'll lose her.

We zip down another flight of stairs to a different line. Next thing I know, we're on a train heading west. I pat the cell in my pocket. Good thinking, Andy. No matter what happens, help's only a call away.

We go three stops, get off without warning, cross the platform to an incoming train headed back where we came from. One stop and we're headed upstairs onto a line going north. We exit in a few minutes, this time for good. I see the station name across the tracks: St. Clair West. Remember the name.

An escalator and we're out on the street in front of a super-sized grocery store. Beside it, a parking lot the size of a football field. Cars and shopping carts everywhere.

The woman moves briskly between the rows of vehicles. She circles, like she's checking to see if the coast is clear. How could anyone have kept up? She slows between two minivans. "Get in the one to the right, side door." She keeps walking.

I glance at the van so I can describe it later, but I'm past the plates and I can't tell models. All I know is, it's gray, dirty, at least a few years old, with tinted windows. Big help that'll be.

I slide the door open. There's a man in a mask. He hauls me inside. The door slams shut. I'm trapped.

"Who—?"

He yanks my hoodie over my shoulders, stuffs my head in a sack, pulls it tight to my neck with a cord.

The driver's door opens, shuts. Who's there? The woman? Someone else?

The van starts up. We're moving.

The man's voice. "You wired?"

"No."

"Strip."

"What?"

"Let's see if you're lying."

I kick off my shoes, pull the hoodie off my arms, and unbutton my shirt.

The van crawls forward. We must be leaving the parking lot. I want to scream for help. But what if they have guns? Knives? They could gut me in a flash.

The van turns right, speeds up.

"You can keep the underwear," the man says, as I fumble with my belt buckle.

We change lanes, turn left. We're going down a hill. Turn right. Go for I don't know how long. Brake. A traffic light? Stop sign? We're moving again, straight ahead.

"He's clean," the man calls out. "No wires. Burn phone in his pocket, though. Better lose it." No, please. I hear a window roll down, picture my cell being dropped. The window goes back up. My pants, hoodie, and shirt are thrown in a ball against my chest. I put them back on as we swing to the left, the right, the right, the left.

Without my eyes, it's hard to figure out what's happening. Each time we accelerate, slow, or turn, my body pitches. How do blind people do it? I plant my feet and press my back against the seat.

The route, Sami. Remember the route. How? What's the distance between turns? How many streets have we passed?

One thing I know: We're out of traffic, into a residential area. We make a bunch more turns, then slow like we're going up an alley or something. We ease to a stop. The driver gets out. I hear a garage door opening. The driver returns. We pull in. The ignition's turned off. The garage door closes. The van doors open.

The man grips me under the armpits. "Careful with

your head." He eases me out. "Keep your eyes on your feet."

He takes the sack off my head.

"There's a path to the house. Don't try anything stupid."

The driver goes first, me second, the man behind. We exit the garage through a makeshift door into a small backyard, and cross a patch of weedy grass. I glimpse a rotting cedar fence on either side, lined with dead flowers and dried-up tomato stalks. We pass an upturned wheelbarrow, a cement birdbath, a couple of dead evergreens.

The back of the house is asphalt shingle siding. There's a porch to the side. We go down a covered cinderblock stairwell to a basement apartment. Inside, there's a smell of mildew coming from an overstuffed pullout couch. Brown stains run up the drywall from the painted cement floor.

The driver—I think it's the woman, can't tell for sure—stands back. The man behind me pushes me forward. "Okay," he says. "You can look up now."

I raise my head. At the back of the low-ceilinged room, there's an open door to a toilet on the left; a counter with a hot plate and sink to the right; in the center, a card table and chairs.

A guy with a scraggly beard is sitting on the fold-up chair behind the table.

It's Tariq Hasan.

Thirty-two

Hasan rises. He looks at me with curiosity and suspicion.

"It's him," Hasan says flatly. "Mohammed Sami Sabiri."

How does he know my full name? Or what I look like? And why did he say it? Did my kidnappers tell him about me? Did they think I might be a plant?

"Yeah, it's me." I jut my jaw, like I'm tough or something. "And you're . . . ." My mouth goes dry.

"Tariq."

Weird. I'm on a first-name basis with a terrorist. That's gotta be Number One on my Ten Things Most Likely Never to Happen list.

Tariq motions me to the chair across from him. "Keep your eyes on me. Don't look back at the others." I picture them with garrotes and machetes. My insides go loose. My knees wobble. I sit.

Then—I don't know how it happens, but it's like I force myself out of my body—I'm not this scared, useless kid anymore. I'm on a mission to find the truth.

"My father told you my name?" The words clear and firm.

Tariq nods. "Your family nickname was Hammed. But you chose Sami after your grandfather."

"What else did he tell you about me?"

"You go to Roosevelt Academy. You're smart, you take chances, you don't listen, you get yourself in trouble." He pauses. "We have a lot in common."

Not on your life.

"Oh, and he's very proud of you," Tariq adds.

"My father? No way."

"Very proud. He says your name and his eyes light up. He calls you a fighter with a good heart and a great future. I admit, he worries about your friends." The smile disappears. "He worried about mine too." A pause. He brightens. "Tea? Biscuits?"

"Sure."

There's a tray on the counter behind him, with biscuits, sugar, milk, spoons, mugs, and a brewed pot of tea. He retrieves it, glancing back at the man and woman. Apparently they don't want any. I stare at the teapot as he pours our mugs. It's shaped like an elephant's head, with the tea coming out of the trunk. He catches me staring.

"Yard sale," he grins.

What, a terrorist with a sense of humor?

"Milk? Sugar?" he asks. "No lemon, I'm afraid."

I want sugar, but I shake my head.

Tariq hands me my mug, takes two spoonfuls of sugar for his own, and stirs slowly. "So you're here." Pause. "How much did your father tell you? How much do you know?"

What do I say? Because it's going to end up with him wanting the package. The package I don't have, because I don't know what it is or where Dad hid it. So do I tell the truth and risk he'll freak out on me? Or do I bluff and hope he'll let something slip?

I play for time. Sip my tea. And have another thought: What if Tariq really *hasn't* escaped? What if the feds have tracked him here and bugged the place. They could be waiting for secret Martyrs to crawl out of the woodwork— like that unidentified terrorist in Meadowvale. If that's the game, and I act like a player, I'll be screwed.

Tariq holds his mug in both hands. "Sami." His eyes go right through me. "I asked you two questions: How much did your father tell you? How much do you know?"

"Depends about what," I shrug.

"Don't play games. The package. Do you have it?" He sips, waits for my answer.

"I . . . I . . ." My tea's going to spill. I put the mug back on the table, and my hands on my lap where he won't see them shake.

"No, I didn't think so," Tariq says. "You didn't come here because of the package."

"Who says?" I whisper. "You have a plan, right? You need it."

Tariq gets up, walks slowly around the table, and rests his hands on the back of my shoulders. "You don't know anything about the package, do you Sami?" he says calmly. "You don't know what's in it. Or why your father packed it."

I shake my head.

"In fact, you don't know anything about anything, do you? You lied to find me. That's a dangerous thing to do. A dangerous, stupid thing, wouldn't you say?" He squeezes my shoulders gently.

The words crawl from my throat. "I guess. Yes."

"Yes," he says, "yes." And he squeezes my shoulders firmly. "So I ask myself, why did you do it? Why are you here?"

This is it. I'm going to die. He's going to strangle me with his bare hands. I'll never see Mom and Dad again. Or Marty and Andy.

"I did it for Dad!" I blurt out. "You made him get that package. I don't know how. But you did, and now he's in trouble, and I wanted the truth so I could save him. He's a good man, a good father, and I've been nothing but trouble. For once I wanted to help. I wanted to make him proud. I love him. So do what you're going to do. Just let him know it's not his fault. Or my buddies' fault. Or anyone's fault but mine."

I wait for the fingers to dig into my neck. For my windpipe to squash, my eyes to bulge out of their sockets. The last thing I'm going to see is that ridiculous elephant's-trunk teapot. Great. Fantastic. Way to screw up a life.

But Tariq pats my shoulders and lets me go. He circles the table twice, then sits down opposite me. "I'm going to tell you a story," he says simply. Then he stares into my eyes, and takes my hands, like I'm a little kid.

"Once," Tariq begins, "there was a boy from Iran. And

264

there was a revolution. The boy's parents supported the revolution, but not what came after. They were thrown in jail. The boy went to live with his grandmother. She slipped him out of Iran, onto a boat to Canada. To Montreal. He was raised by friends of friends of family friends."

"I've heard this story," I say slowly.

"Some of it, some of it," Tariq nods. "The boy grew into a smart, handsome young man. He worked hard and did well. The friends of family friends helped him to go to university, a university named McGill. He married their eldest daughter, Neda. He told himself it was love. But it was duty."

"No." My neck tingles. "It was love."

Tariq hushes me with a quiet shake of his head. "It was love, later, yes. But back then, it was duty and obligation in a noisy rooming house, and each of them working two jobs, and going to school and more school and more school and no way out. And the young man felt trapped."

My heart's bursting: "What did he do?"

"In his final year at the university, he met a research assistant who worked for one of his professors in the Biology department. Her name was Yasmin. She was from Egypt. And some nights when the young man's wife was away at work, he and Yasmin would get together. They shared dreams. They shared everything."

"But he stayed with Neda," I say firmly.

Tariq nods. "He won a postgraduate scholarship in microbiology to NYU. What was he to do? Break with the woman who'd helped him achieve success? No. He left his heart, and went with Neda to the United States. Yasmin broke all contact. She never replied to his letters, refused all phone calls. And a month later, when she discovered she was pregnant, she kept the news to herself."

"Pregnant?"

"For the sake of her family's honor, she moved to Toronto. She wore a ring, spoke of a husband who'd passed away, and never dated again."

Silence. I'm afraid to know what I already guess. "You said this woman, Yasmin, was pregnant," I whisper. "Was there a baby?"

Tariq rests his hands on the table, palms up.

My head whirrs. "You're . . . I'm . . . I'm your . . ."

"Yes," he says.

I stare across the table at my half brother. My half brother. Tariq Hasan is my half brother. My half brother. I think the words over and over. Nothing connects. I'm floating. Numb.

"A year ago, my mother died of breast cancer," Tariq

says gently. "Before she died, she told me the truth. She said it was important I have the chance to know about my father. 'Father? What father?' I thought. 'I never had a father. Why would I want to see some stranger who ruined Mom's life?' Going through her things, I found articles she'd printed off the Internet. Stories of his success. End of the summer, my curiosity got the better of me. I wrote him a letter telling him all about me. That I existed, for a start." He chuckles, but not like it's funny. "First letter I've ever written. Like, with an actual stamp and everything. Then again, it's not the sort of thing you e-mail."

"That's when Dad told you he was coming to Toronto?"

Tariq nods. "We met at the library opposite my place. I think you've been there? We had supper. Then went to the Leafs on Friday, the Jays on Saturday."

I swallow hard. Those were *my* games.

"We talked forever," Tariq says. "He went on and on about you, showed me pictures of you that he keeps in his wallet."

"Dad keeps pictures of me in his wallet?"

"There's you as a baby. Cute kid, what happened?" he teases. "There's you graduating from elementary school, and a photo of you at an Eid celebration in front of your mosque."

"I never knew." It's like I'm seeing another Dad.

"He asked about my life," Tariq continues. "I showed him shots of me with my buddies camping and playing paintball; of me and my girlfriend at Wonderland. I told him my plans for art school. He said he thought my buddies looked rough—which is true—and that art school was crazy, but I should follow my dreams."

"I can't imagine Dad telling me to follow my dreams."

"Yeah, well," Tariq smiles, "he was meeting me for the first time. What else could he say?" He sighs. "After the final Jays game, I wasn't sure what I was feeling, but I didn't want it to be over, to have him disappear again, forever. I told him I wanted to see where he lived and worked, to meet you all. You people are the only blood I have. Mom's folks are gone. Her brothers and sisters, my aunts and uncles—when they found out why she'd left Montreal, they disowned us. I've never met my cousins. They're kinda traditional, eh?"

"What did Dad say about coming?"

"He panicked. 'You stay away,' he said. 'I have a happy family. I won't have it destroyed.' I asked if maybe he could get me some pictures of his parents—my grandparents. Or of my great-grandma who helped him escape, or maybe of the ancestral home in Iran.

Or any cards, notes, or letters Mom might have sent him from before they broke up. Any medical history that might come in handy. Any mementos. It was all 'No, no, no'—an ugly end to a magic weekend. Then, just before the raid, I get this e-mail about how he's packed the stuff I want, and how he'll show me around Rochester after all. He was so nervous in Toronto; he must've been a basket case at home."

I nod. Poor Dad. That's why he wouldn't let Mom and me go with him to Toronto. Why he said there were things he couldn't tell me. Why he acted so strange. It explains that e-mail the prosecution read in court.

Forgive me, Dad. You were trying to protect me. To protect Mom. As for the stuff you did when you were young—how can I judge what you did before I was born? That's between you and Mom.

Mom. What'll you say—what'll you feel—if you find out? *When* you find out. Because you've *got* to find out. It's the only way to prove Dad innocent.

Thirty-three

I need something to help me focus. I take a biscuit.

"Tariq," I say, "if Dad wasn't bringing you anything dangerous, if he was just packing family photos and mementos—then there was never a terror plot."

"No kidding, there was never a plot!"

"So give yourself up. Tell the authorities what you know. If you and Dad speak up, you'll go free."

"Oh really?" snorts the man behind me. "You watch the news?"

Tariq puts up his hand. The man goes quiet.

"If I give myself up, who'll believe me?" Tariq says. "No one, and you know it. I'd need the letter I sent him. And the package he made for me. Does he have them?"

"They would've been in his office. They'll be with all his stuff at the FBI."

"Exactly. They'll be classified. Buried. Meanwhile I'm damned by all those photos and cell videos of me and the so-called Brotherhood of Martyrs. If they don't nail me for the bio plot, they'll nail me for something else. I'll never get out. Goddamn Erim Malik!"

Without warning, Tariq's on his feet, fists smashing the card table. One of the legs buckles. I save the teapot, but everything else goes flying.

Tariq slumps against the counter. His friends must be stepping forward, because he waves them away. "Stay back! Sami mustn't see you. You're in enough trouble." He slides to the floor, presses his elbows to his knees, his hands over his head. He's gulping air fast.

I don't know what I should do. What I *do* do is sit cross-legged in front of him. Tariq settles, his breaths deep but controlled.

"We were just a bunch of guys," he says. "Most of us unemployed or back in school. A few of us had old cars. Only three or four of us had girlfriends. Some days, we'd meet up at mosque for morning prayers, then go to the country to a paintball range, get dressed up in camouflage gear, horse around. Other days, maybe we'd catch a flick.

We were a losers' club."

He wipes an eye with his wrist. "Anyway, my buddy Abdul Malik had a cousin Erim. Erim talked the talk, all right—sharia this, sharia that—but I knew he did coke, and he'd roughed up a few kids, and there were rumors he was forging passports at his uncle's copy shop. But he was Abdul's family, so we let him tag along. We didn't know how to say no."

I stare at the floor, a little scared. I know all about being afraid to say no. What if I was Tariq?

Tariq continues. "End of the summer, we're in some field having a few beers after paintball. I know, I know, alcohol's haraam; but that's what we were doing. Erim's taking a video of us with his cell, and he makes some crack about us whining all the time. 'Yeah, you're all a bunch of martyrs,' he says. 'A brotherhood of martyrs.' And I go, 'That's us, the Brotherhood of Martyrs.' And we all laugh, 'Great name,' and joke that we should make T-shirts or something. Only that part's not on TV, is it?"

I shake my head.

"So then Erim takes out a gun, and we're like, 'Whoa, Erim, cut it out, this is Canada.' But he just lines up a few beer bottles, and says target practice is fun, and what's the big deal? And we're in this field in the middle of nowhere, so we think, yeah, maybe he's right, why not? And each of us takes a shot or two—and we're lousy shots let me tell you—and Erim makes a video with his cell, so we can laugh about it later he says."

Tariq squeezes his hands on his knees. "This goes on a few weeks, Erim taking videos of this and that. Sometimes he talks up how bad things are, how somebody should just blow up the works—not for real, you know, just like a figure of speech—and we're joking, 'Yeah, Parliament, *boom*! The CN Tower, *boom*! Port-o-potties on the midway, *boom*!' 'What about the prime minister?' Erim says. 'Off with his head,' I joke with a big wave, like that character in *Alice in Wonderland*. I mean it was stupid talk, totally bogus—not like it sounds on TV."

And I think of Eddy's video, and all the other stuff in my life that looks one way but isn't, or the way things have looked with Andy and Marty and they weren't.

"When your father . . . our father . . . when he said he was coming to Toronto, I was so excited," Tariq says. "I told my friends about him, how important he was. It made me feel important, just saying it. I built it all up, the category four stuff. I said how he was so important he could move toxic shit whenever, wherever he wanted. I was flying so high. The guys were happy for me. They knew I didn't have a dad; Montreal's not so far, people move, they gossip. Well anyway, now I had a dad, and he was a big deal."

"Till you destroyed him." A dam breaks inside my head. "Dad—*my* dad—he's in jail. My family's trashed. Because you, a total stranger, had to find your goddamn roots."

"I'm sorry. I'm sorry."

"You're sorry?" I yell. "Maybe it's not your fault, but you're *sorry*?"

He lowers his head in shame. "Want to get madder?"

"You bet."

"Here's the kicker: Erim Malik, the weasel with the gun, the dirt bag who got us talking, who made the videos, who pushes drugs and beats on kids—he's the only one of us who never got arrested."

"What?"

"You heard me," Tariq says bitterly. "He's walking free. Word is, he's a paid government informant. Star witness for the prosecution."

At dusk, Tariq has his friends blindfold me and drop me at a subway on the Yonge line. I take it down to the square opposite the Eaton Centre, the plaza Andy marked for our rendezvous.

When the guys see me, they do a two-man pile-on.

"We came so close to calling the cops," they babble. "Like, we were so scared, man. You okay? What did they do to you?"

"I'm fine. Everything's cool."

"I almost got arrested for hopping the turnstile," Andy says.

"And I got a bruise the color of eggplant for smashing into it!" Marty exclaims.

"By the time we got back outside, the Chevy'd been towed," Andy moans. "It cost more to get it back than it's worth. But who cares? You're here! You're alive!"

A few minutes later, we're on a bench by a fountain, stuffing our faces with fries.

"Andy," I say, "I need your cell. There's something I need to do."

"You're calling the cops?"

"I have nothing to tell them—not yet," I say. "But this morning I made Mom a promise."

Whoever's bugged our home will trace my call and know I'm phoning from a cell tower in Toronto. So I don't call Mom directly.

"Mr. Bernstein?"

"Sami?"

"Yeah, it's me. I need a big favor. Could you please go over to my place? The house is probably wired, so ask Mom to step outside. Tell her I'm safe, I'm sorry if she's worried, and I'll be home by tomorrow, noon. Also, please tell her I need to see Mr. Bhanjee immediately."

Thirty-four

Mom and Mr. Bhanjee are watching from the bay window when we pull in. Before my foot hits the pavement, Mom's in the driveway. "Where were you?" doesn't begin to cover it. First, she hugs me so hard I think my ribs'll crack. Then, she's shaking me. I thought last night's visit from Mr. Bernstein would have settled her down, but the cloak-and-dagger stuff about having to go outside to talk just made it worse. Not to mention me saying I needed to see our lawyer.

"What have you done?"

"Nothing," I say. Which isn't exactly true, but I'm not gonna pull an Oprah on our front lawn.

The three of us sit in the patio chairs in the backyard.

I don't say anything about Dad's affair or him being Tariq's father, but I spill the rest: how I met Tariq, how Erim Malik is this slimeball into guns and drugs and passport forgery who set everybody up. Mom's knuckles are so white I half expect the metal armrests she's holding to snap. I'm sure not looking forward to when Mr. Bhanjee leaves.

I wrap up my story. Mr. Bhanjee beams. "Your information about Malik is pure gold," he says. "It's surely no coincidence that he's the government's star witness. A little digging, and I suspect we'll find that he's also their informant. Most likely, he was about to be arrested for the things you mentioned, and cut himself a deal: If charges against him were dropped, he'd turn in a terrorist cell."

"That's why he started getting everyone to mouth off on video," I say. "He framed innocent people, so he could go free."

"I see that kind of thing all the time, in all sorts of cases." Mr. Bhanjee nods. "What can you expect when prosecutors offer criminals favors and plea bargains to act as informants and witnesses?"

"But even without Malik, Dad has a problem: his e-mail, the one they read in court about him preparing a package for Tariq. But I have good news there too. I can show it was innocent." I pause. "Mom, sorry, I can only say what it was really about to Mr. Bhanjee."

"I already know what it was about," Mom says. She smoothes her skirt, presses her hands on her thighs, and looks me in the eye. "Tariq Hasan is your father's son. Your half brother."

My jaw drops.

"Mr. Bhanjee and I visited your father Tuesday," Mom says. "It's what gave me the migraine. He told me that Hasan wrote him a letter of introduction before he went to Toronto. And how later he searched through boxes in the storage room for photographs and mementos to make Hasan a package about the family, while I was watching golf on TV."

I look down, barely able to speak. The patio stones swim in front of my eyes. "What's going to happen . . . with you and Dad?"

Mom nudges her chair beside mine. She strokes the hair over my ear. "Montreal was a long time ago. I had a feeling, back then, that something was wrong. But after we moved here, that feeling went away. I've never felt it since." She cups my face with her hands. "It was hard for your father to tell me. He was sure I'd leave and take you with me."

The words choke from my throat. "Are you going to?"

"I thought about it," Mom says. "But I told him the past is the past, and that I love him." A smile flickers across her lips. "I also said if he did it again, I'd yank out his beard, shove it down his throat, and let the devil choke him."

An awkward pause. Mr. Bhanjee breaks it. "Your father's told the authorities that he's Hasan's father. DNA testing on Hasan, or hairs from his apartment, can prove their genetic connection. But Hasan's letter of introduction was the best evidence that your dad had just discovered their relationship, and that the package he referred to in his e-mail contained nothing more sinister than family pictures."

"So now that they have Hasan's letter, they'll let Dad go?"

"No." Mom shudders. "The thing is, they don't have it. Hasan's letter is missing."

"It's what? Don't tell me. Dad got rid of it, didn't he? He was scared we'd find it. So he ripped it up. He burned it!"

"Not quite," Mr. Bhanjee says. "But just as bad. He hid it. Now it's gone."

Mom hits her chest with her fist. "The FBI. They

destroyed it when they tore the place apart. I'm sure of it. We'll never see it again."

"Where did Dad hide it?" I whisper.

"In his office. Behind a framed photograph of the two of you. 'The one place my sons could be together,' he said."

My heart skips. "Wait right here!"

And I race downstairs and reach under my bed. The broken glass falls free of the frame. Sure enough, under the picture of Dad and me—Tariq's letter, dated, and neatly folded with a small, signed graduation photo.

I give it to Mom and Mr. Bhanjee. Mom covers her mouth.

"Mom, if I hadn't gone to Toronto and found out about Tariq, would you ever have told me?"

She shakes her head, wiping her eyes. "Your father made me promise not to. 'What's the point?' he said. 'Without Tariq's letter, it's hopeless. Better, at least, we save our pride.'"

"So the letter would never have been found. It would have stayed a secret right under our noses. Dad could have gone to prison forever because of fear and shame."

Mr. Bhanjee interrupts. "I'll see that this is copied and placed in evidence," he says, putting it in his briefcase. "In the meantime, Sami, it's still too early for celebration."

"But we've proved there's no terror cell."

"Not quite," Mr. Bhanjee says. "All we've shown is that Tariq is your father's son, that the package mentioned in your father's e-mail was personal, and that Erim Malik got his friends to say things on video. But the fact that Tariq and your father had personal dealings *doesn't* prove they weren't also engaged in a terrorist conspiracy. And simply because people are coaxed into saying things doesn't make the things they say untrue."

"But there's got to be a reason for suspicion."

"There is," Mr. Bhanjee says. "Remember the court announcement of the unidentified terrorist? Someone else from this area, besides your father, made repeated attempts to contact the Brotherhood. What are the odds that a second person from this community would know the same group of unemployed youths in Toronto? Or that he and your father wouldn't know each other? If the connection is innocent, why won't any of the Brotherhood identify him? The coincidence and the silence are suspicious and alarming."

"So what can we do?" I gulp.

"I'm not sure," Mr. Bhanjee says. "But before your father can go free, the government will want satisfactory answers to two questions. First: Who is the mystery contact? Second: What is his or her link to your father and the Brotherhood?"

"The FBI have started interviewing people at the mosque," Mom says. "People whose thinking is extreme."

I flash on something Mr. Bernstein would say: "Thoughts aren't crimes. If they were, everyone on Earth would be in jail."

"I'm not saying anything"—Mom hesitates—"but you know Mr. Ibrahim? A while back, he was strip-searched in Newark. His name was on a list. Maybe there was a reason after all."

"Stop it!" I yell. "That's the kind of talk that got Dad in trouble."

"I'm not accusing him," Mom says. "But Mr. Bhanjee's questions need answers."

Suddenly, out of nowhere, those questions and answers explode in my head. How does stuff happen? How do little things cross the line into something big and terrible?

I struggle to control my voice. "Mr. Bhanjee, have the authorities said which member of the Brotherhood the unidentified terrorist tried to contact?"

"No," he says. "The information is classified."

"I'll bet it was Tariq."

"Why? What are you getting at?" Mr. Bhanjee frowns.

"When Dad went to Toronto, I thought he was having an affair. I spied on him to find out, found Tariq's number on his computer. I phoned it from the multiplex at the mall. I phoned it again the next day from the mosque. The only person apart from the FBI who'd know what number was called, when and from where, is the person who made the calls. Well, I've told you. So write it down, Mr. Bhanjee. Make it legal. Let them check. The so-called secret terrorist is me."

Thirty-five

The case against Dad turns into confetti. The FBI never says who the "unidentified terrorist" tried to contact, or how or when. That information remains Classified For Reasons Of National Security. Also For Reasons Of Nobody Wants To Look Like An Idiot.

What matters is, as soon as the authorities see my affidavit and interview me, they search the hard drive history in Dad's computer and the one I used at the Academy, to see how I figured out Tariq's phone number and address. Then they check the places and times I called him. Suddenly, the "unidentified terrorist" is downgraded to a "person of interest." And within a week, they announce that the "person of interest" has been cleared, and that whole part of the case disappears—as if everyone decides to have amnesia, and they're on to other things.

Such as the official investigation at Shelton Laboratories. The lab has reopened, so the report must have been completed. The press wants to know when it'll be released. The government says, "No comment." But the press demands to know what materials went missing, and what was found on the surveillance tapes. The government's answer: "Sorry. Top secret."

"If anything was missing from the inventory, we'd have heard about it," Mr. Bhanjee tells Mom and me, leaning against the desk in his office. "The fact that we haven't means that every last petri dish has been accounted for. Which proves your father didn't take anything from the lab for Tariq. That, coupled with Tariq's letter, makes your father's explanation of his e-mail airtight."

"So why don't they admit it?" I say. "Why do they keep holding him? It's like they know Dad is innocent but they don't care. They're going to hold him forever just so they won't have to admit they made a mistake." I want to smash something big time. But then *I'd* be in trouble, only for something real, and that's the last thing Mom needs.

"Breathe," Mr. Bhanjee tells us. "They can't hold Arman forever. The press will keep pushing to get that report released. I'll do the same in court. Sooner or later, pressure will force out the truth, and the prosecution will find that pursuing a case without evidence is more embarrassing than your father's release. The longer a wrongfully accused is held, the greater the public outrage."

"Oh yeah?" I say. "Call someone a terrorist and nobody gives a shit."

"Sami!" Mom exclaims.

"It's true, Mom, and you know it. Especially for people like us."

Mom squeezes my hand. "It's hard, I know. But it's just a matter of waiting. I've taken a second mortgage on the house. The money will see us through till this is resolved. Don't worry."

I'm not worried. I'm angry.

To keep my mind off things—not to mention because I have to—I go back to school. This time, I'm with Andy and Marty at Meadowvale Secondary. It feels strange in the halls sometimes, people staring at me and pretending not to, but the guys keep me sane. After class, we like to hit Mr. Softy's. The city's drained the water from the fountain across the street for the winter, but on sunny days it's still warm enough to sit out on the ledge.

That's where we are now, eating ice cream, sharing stupid secrets. Like the one about my name. "Remember when we first met?" I say. "I was so ashamed of who I was, I let you think my name was English: Sammy, spelled S-A-M-M-Y. Well, it's not. It's Arabic: Sami, spelled S-A-M-I."

"Some secret." Andy laughs. "You think we never saw the class register?"

I feel so dumb I burst out laughing. It's good to laugh. It makes the crap disappear, if only for a second.

Marty's ice cream drips down his cone and over his fingers. "Hey," he licks his hand, "what's with those guys over there in the BMW and the SUV?"

I look across the street. And feel sick. I've tried to forget about the Academy. But it's not like it disappeared. It's not like Eddy Duh Turd's disappeared either. He and his gang are staring at us.

"You know the Academy thugs I told you about?"

Marty's cone crumbles; his ice cream falls to the pavement. "One of those guys is Eddy Duh Turd?"

"You got it. Driver's seat, BMW."

"What do they want?"

"Guess."

Andy gets up nice and slow. He sticks his hand in his jeans. Fishing for the keys to the Deathmobile, I figure. "Want to make a run for it?"

I shake my head. "You guys can. It's me they're after. I'm not running. Not anymore."

"But there's six of them."

"There'll always be six of them."

Eddy sees us looking at him. He and his goons pile out of the cars.

"Yo, sand monkey, I've been looking for you," Eddy calls out as they swagger across the street. "You trying to hide? Your ass may be expelled, but you still answer to me. Got it?"

I step forward. "Get off my case, Harrison."

"Or what?" Eddy mocks. "You'll cry on me? Figures we'd find you here. Mr. *Softy*'s. Perfect."

Andy and Marty move beside me. I motion them back.

"This your crew?" Eddy sneers. He casually kicks a stone in my direction. "How's your daddy? He like the showers at the jail? You should maybe introduce him to your pal, Bernstein."

Eddy's friends make kissing sounds.

"You gonna take that?" Eddy dares. "You pissing your pants, maybe?" He glances at Andy and Marty. "Did your girlfriend ever tell you he had his head in a shit bowl? Yeah, he's a regular shit-for-brains."

His buddies laugh.

And out of nowhere, I'm filled with this weird tingling, this power. I can't describe it. All I know is, I'm not afraid. I'm not mad. In fact, I'm scary-calm. "Yeah, Eddy, I had my head in a toilet," I say. "But I didn't put it there. You did. Only the crud of the crud would do a thing like that." I look Eddy square in the eye. "As long as you live, you'll remember that day. You'll know what you did to me. And you'll know what that makes you."

Eddy rears his head back. "What, you think you're better than me? You got expelled. Your dad's Dr. Death. The stink of your name will follow you forever. Me, I've got it made. I'll be at my old man's Ivy League. Or go straight to the family firm."

"That's the other thing. No matter how big you get, you'll never know if it's because of you or your dad. That's gotta hurt. I feel sorry for you, Eddy."

"What?" he sputters. "You don't get to feel sorry for me!"

"Can't help it." I shrug.

"Oh, you'll help it all right," Eddy says. His buddies close in around us. He raises his fists.

"Go ahead," I say. "Beat the shit out of me. What'll that prove? Nothing. Except I'm right about you. So go ahead, Eddy. Prove me right."

Eddy doesn't know what to do. It's like he's facing a crazy person or something. He drops his fists. "Asshole," he says. "Come on guys, these pussies aren't worth it." He backs across the street, giving us the finger. Then he and his crew jump into their cars and take off, horns blaring.

"Good luck, Eddy," I murmur. "You'll need it."

Thirty-six

It finally happens late one Friday afternoon. Mr. Bhanjee calls from the jail. "They're letting Arman go. I'll drive him home." The FBI has prepared a brief statement of apology, like they did with the man in Portland who was falsely accused of being a member of Al Quaeda based on a quarter of a fingerprint. The apology is nice, but all I care about is Dad.

His release has been kept quiet, "out of respect for the family's privacy," according to the authorities. "The real reason," Mr. Bhanjee says, "is because the truth makes them look bad. Late Friday is when officials dump stories that could embarrass them. Offices are closed or closing, so the press has a hard time getting reactions for the evening news, and hardly anybody pays attention to things over the weekend. By Monday the world's moved on; if there's any fallout, it's diluted."

I wish the media was as loud about advertising people's innocence as it is about accusing them. Still, I have to admit, the last thing I want right now is a bunch of cameras in our face.

The street's totally quiet when Dad arrives. Mom and I stay by the bay window, afraid to do anything to cause a scene. Dad gets out of the car. Mr. Bhanjee waits to leave till he's made his way to the front door.

Dad moves stiffly, as if he's frozen and the tiniest move will break his joints. He closes the door behind him.

Mom's suddenly beside him. She holds him tight, stroking his back with her hands. They rock together, whispering each other's names.

Finally Mom steps aside. "Your son," she says.

Dad stands there, lost.

I take a step toward him.

He raises his arms to hug me, then looks away in shame.

"I never wanted this for you," he says.

"I know, Dad."

"I never wanted that you or your mother should know."

"I know."

His voice breaks. "I wanted to be a good father. A perfect father. I wanted to save you from my mistakes. My weakness. Forgive me."

"Dad," I say. "You're Dad. That's all I want. Dad."

And I go to him, wrap my arms around him.

"Sami. My son. My Sami."

Apart from school, I stay close to home. Dad's taking a long vacation before returning to work, and I want to be near if he needs me. He's good during the day; at night, not so much. I keep my door open, so I can hear when he's up with nightmares. Those times, I go to the kitchen and sit with him while he has his warm milk and molasses. What happened to him in jail was rough. The reaction of former friends hurts too.

"We'll get through this," he says, like I'm a friend as well as his son. "The neighbors didn't want us when we first came here. That went away. It's back again. But not forever. We're Sabiris. We don't run."

I'm glad Dad's my dad. He's brave. All things considered, we have it lucky. Not like the Brotherhood. It takes more than a year for them to even get to trial. In the end, there aren't any terror charges, but the video evidence gets them convicted of smaller things, like illegal discharge of a firearm and uttering death threats. The ones on expired student visas get deported; the ones who were landed immigrants get their status revoked; the rest get time served.

Tariq takes a bigger hit. When he turned himself in, he not only got nailed for all the small stuff, but for public mischief and interfering with a police investigation as well; he gets six months on top. His girlfriend and a buddy go down for harboring a fugitive; they get a year's probation.

The scary thing is what happens to Erim Malik. Nothing. Absolutely nothing.

Prosecutors never go back on a deal; they're afraid if they did that informants would stop talking. So despite the fact that Malik is obviously a public menace, he gets a free pass. He'll be watched, but for how long? And sure, his uncle's copy shop is closed, but who knows what happened to all the fake passports he fenced before the cops came calling? Maybe some went to harmless illegals: nannies or day laborers. But the others? Thinking about it gives me chills.

Anyway—Tariq. We've visited him in jail. Mom too. I thought it'd be weird, but Mom has a heart that won't stop. "I hear you're my stepson," she smiled. And it was like he'd been family forever.

Tariq will never live near us or anything. With his record, I don't think he can even get into the country. But I like the idea of having an older brother. I'm so glad we met.

I dream of the day that he's free.

I picture Dad, Mom, and me renting a cottage near Toronto. We invite the guys. We invite Tariq too. I picture us having a barbecue, kicking back, and teasing Dad into the lake for a swim. I picture us watching the sun go down, laughing and talking around a campfire, till my folks go to bed and we fall asleep on the sand.

It's a beautiful dream.

And one day, I know it's going to happen.

Thanks

I am filled with enormous gratitude to the many people who helped me with the cultural and legal details in *Borderline*.

Within the Muslim community, I am particularly indebted to members of the Noor Cultural Centre in Toronto, especially executive committee member Faizal Kayum and his wife, Laila Baksh, and their son, Azeem Kayum; and to the former Noor Chair at York University, Professor Timothy Gianotti. I am also grateful to Yassir Hakim, science teacher at Collège français, Toronto, and to journalist and documentary producer Sadia Zaman.

On legal matters, I consulted New York attorney Stephen Watt of the American Civil Liberties Union;

Stephen M. Perlitsch, an attorney engaged in American immigration law; and Paul Copeland, who argued the law on detention certificates before the Canadian Supreme Court.

I am also grateful for the time and assistance of Barry Rosen, press attaché to the American embassy in Tehran during the 1979–1981 hostage crisis; Margaret McPhedran Axford, regional manager with Canadian Border Services; former private investigator Stephen Dow; TASC's Michael Behrens; American educators Frances Shoonmaker and Liesl Bolin; Reverend Gene Bolin; and the *Toronto Star*'s editor emeritus Haroon Siddiqui, international affairs columnist Thomas Walkom, and national security reporter Michelle Shephard.

Last, but not least, my deepest thanks to my editors, Lynne Missen, Susan Rich, Sarah Howden, Beate Schaefer, and Catherine Onder; and to my reading circle: Daniel Legault, Louise Baldacchino, Christine Baldacchino, and Vickie Stewart.